OSWAIN AND THE MYSTERY OF THE STAR STONE

For Mark

Oswain
and the
Mystery of the
Star Stone

JOHN HOUGHTON

KINGSWAY PUBLICATIONS
EASTBOURNE

ISBN 0 85476 968 4

Published by
KINGSWAY PUBLICATIONS
Lottbridge Drove, Eastbourne, BN23 6NT, England.
Email: books@kingsway.co.uk

Book design and production for the publishers by
Bookprint Creative Services, P.O. Box 827, BN21 3YJ, England.
Printed in Great Britain by Cox & Wyman Ltd, Reading, Berkshire.

Contents

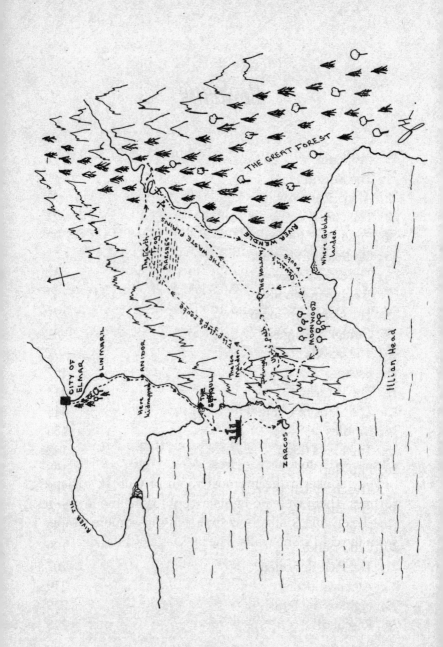

Prologue

Gold, lots of shiny bright gold, glittered in the flickering candlelight.

A fat green goblin sat cross-legged in the midst of his treasure. He ran his bony fingers through a pile of precious stones. His name was Gublak and his eyes were greedy with desire, as only a goblin's can be.

'Such pretty things,' he breathed. 'So shiny and so – mine! You are all mine.' He licked his hungry green lips as he drooled over his hoard. Then his eyes hardened. 'But you are not enough. There is something more that I want – and I intend to have it.'

A soft knock on the door followed by a call from one of his servants disturbed his thoughts.

'I humbly beg your pardon, your Eminence, but the visitor has arrived.'

The goblin grunted and with reluctance left his treasure in order to meet his guest.

They spoke in the topmost room of Gublak's island fortress. There were no lights except for the moon and it cast heavy black shadows that hung in sombre drapes from the cold stone walls. The air was as still as death.

'I believe the time is near and soon you shall have your heart's desire,' said the visitor.

Gublak's eyes gleamed in the moonlight. When he spoke his voice was husky. 'Good. If what you say is true, your reward shall be great. Tell me what you know.'

The mysterious visitor unfolded his dark scheme.

'It will not be difficult to take her captive,' he concluded.

'Excellent, excellent!' The goblin paced the room, rubbing his hands together. 'Then it will be mine. How I have desired that jewel! You bring good news tonight and I am well pleased.' He turned sharply on his guest. 'But I warn you, do not fail me now. I must possess that magic stone. Failure means death. Do you understand?'

'I shall not fail you,' the visitor answered. 'If all the preparations are made according to plan, nothing can go wrong.'

Gublak nodded curtly. The interview was over and the visitor departed as silently as he had come. Far below, the desolate howl of a wolf chilled the night air.

* * *

Oswain stirred fitfully in his sleep. Something was nagging at his mind and he began to dream.

He saw a glistening transparent jewel that floated on a dark green sea. A storm was brewing and it broke suddenly and with such violence that the fury of the waves seemed about to swamp the fragile gem. Then, just as it seemed lost, the peak of an ice-capped mountain arose from the raging sea and carried the precious stone to safety. Higher and higher it climbed until the sea was out of sight. Then the jewel burst into a brilliant blue light that shone like a star from the top of the mountain, and Oswain saw his own hands, raised, and touched by the light.

He awoke with a start.

Not long after, in the cold hour before dawn, he journeyed to Elmere, the Star-Pool that lay in the Enchanted Glade of the Great Forest of Alamore, over which he ruled. Here was set the Merestone whose power gave life to the forest. The fragrance of the air and the energy that flowed from the Merestone cleared Oswain's head and cheered his heart. Yet the unease that had broken his sleep remained with him.

'Elmesh, guide me,' he whispered as he gazed into the gently glowing Star-Pool. For a moment he saw simply his own reflection. Then the waters swirled and he saw the face of a young princess. She seemed to be in much distress and the howling of wolves filled Oswain's mind.

'Alena!' he breathed.

* * *

Terror, in the form of a deadly hawk, hovered over the northern Cadaelin Mountains. Not a bird was safe, and especially not turtle doves flying from west to east. Only those that crossed the mountains by flying farther south could hope to avoid the peril, but not all of these would escape unscathed – and much would turn on the fate of one such bird.

Far away, Brankleshanks struggled to his feet and

reached for a powerful crossbow. The arrow he fired flew straight and true. He had practised enough. It was time for action.

1

The Round Hole

'It's very deep,' declared Sarah.

'Yes, and no fence around it either,' said her elder brother, Peter. 'I wouldn't like to be walking across here in the dark.'

'Just imagine, though,' said Andrew, the youngest of the three. 'You could be running across the grass chased by a ferocious tiger and suddenly you see this in front of you and you swerve out of the way at the last minute and the tiger goes "Aaagh!" and crashes to its doom.'

'There aren't any tigers in England,' retorted his brother.

'What about in safari parks?'

'But not here in Cornwall.'

'I bet there are.'

'Oh, shush, you two!' said Sarah.

The three Brown children – Peter, Sarah and Andrew – were on holiday with their parents at a small Cornish village called Trevone. Peter was twelve and he had just finished an interesting year seven at school by accidentally head-butting his form tutor, Mr Pyle, in the stomach while playing a game of blindfold bulls and matadors with his mates. Mr Pyle, not for the first time in Peter's experience, had entered the classroom at just the wrong moment. Since it was the last afternoon of term, he had sent Peter home with a letter for his parents recommending that when the boy left school he should consider becoming a battering ram since he seemed incapable of using his head for anything better!

However, all that was forgotten once they had set off for their holidays, though his nine-year-old brother, Andrew, kept calling him 'Pyle driver' and was using Peter's Manchester United shirt as a matador's cloak. Andrew could be a bit of a pain at times, but mostly they got on well together. Today they both wore shorts and T-shirts and trainers. Their ten-year-old sister, Sarah, wore shorts and a pink crop top. She had wanted her belly button pierced but her horrified mother had said, 'No. Not until you're sixteen, *at least*!' So instead, Sarah had drawn a gold ring and a diamond on her tummy with felt tip pens, which she thought was rather cool because then she could have a different one every day if she wanted.

All three were staring down a huge round hole sunk into the low northern cliff of the sandy inlet and about twenty-five metres from its edge. The hole – one of a number on the north Cornish coast – was some thirty-five metres across and as many deep. At the bottom of this particular one ran an arched tunnel of dripping rock that led to the sea. The children planned to climb down the steep track that led to the bottom of the hole and then work their way through the slippery tunnel out on to the rocky coastline.

Peter went first and slithered rapidly to the bottom. Sarah followed more cautiously.

'Hurry up,' urged Andrew from behind her.

'I'm doing my best,' she gasped. 'Don't rush me or I'll fall. This feels dangerous.'

'You're doing fine,' Peter shouted, deciding to be big brother in charge. 'Come on, it's all right.'

A couple of minutes later Sarah and Andrew slid down the last few metres and joined him.

'Wow, it doesn't half make you grubby,' said Andrew, studying his dirty hands and the seat of his shorts.

'Just mind you don't wipe them on your T-shirt or you'll be in trouble from Mum,' his sister retorted. 'You know how she moans about doing washing on holiday.'

'Let's go through the tunnel,' said Peter. He indicated the split rock ahead of them.

'Come on then,' cried Andrew. He raced off, but soon slowed down for the others when he found out the hard way just how slippery the sea-washed rocks were.

They picked their way along the passage, shouting as they went to make their voices boom off the damp walls and trying to keep their feet dry, though it was too late for Andrew who just sloshed through the pools. The tunnel brought them out onto a wild coast of close-packed broken rocks between which ran the sea. Behind them stood the sheer cliff face of the Cornish coastline.

'Hey, let's go rock hopping,' said Andrew. 'The tide's still low, so we've plenty of time.'

The others agreed and for the next quarter of an hour they enjoyed themselves clambering over the barnacled rocks.

In fact, they were having so much fun that not one of them noticed the silent mist seeping across the sea towards them. At least, not until Peter suddenly realised he could no longer see Sarah, and the air had turned cold.

'What's happened? Andrew, Sarah, where are you?'

'Over here.' Their voices sounded muffled in the mist.

Although it took only a couple of minutes to find one another, even after such a short time the mist had grown so thick that the cliff was now no more than a dim shadow behind them.

'We'd better get back, I think,' Peter muttered anxiously. 'Come on.'

They groped their way towards the cliff, but discovered to their dismay that they could no longer find the entrance to the tunnel.

'That's funny. I'm sure it was here,' said Peter.

'Well, we've lost it, haven't we?' Andrew replied. 'What are we going to do now?'

'Only one thing for it. We'll have to follow the cliff until we come to the beach. Let's just hope these rocks go all the way round and we don't have to swim for it,' Peter answered.

'I feel a bit scared,' Sarah confessed. 'It feels really odd, this mist. Who'd have thought it – in the middle of summer?' She shivered, and she knew it wasn't just because of the cold.

2
Alena Runs Away

'I'm fed up with everything!'

Princess Alena's private bedroom overlooked the splendid palace gardens. Beyond lay the fine white buildings of the City of Elmar, capital of the West and home to the royal family. The summer air was warm, the scent of honeysuckle sweet and the flower beds a celebration of bright colours; but this did nothing to lessen the princess's foul mood.

She sat on the broad sill of the lattice window kicking her heels against the wall.

'I mean, look at it all,' she continued. 'Same old room, same old days. Get up, get dressed, be on my best behaviour. Meet the guests. Smile at everyone. I'm sick and tired of smiling! Why can't I do something different?'

The princess was not talking to herself. Perched on the back of a chair was a large black crow who listened, bright eyed, to everything she said.

She dropped down from the window sill and wandered over to the wardrobe mirror where she scowled at her reflection. The princess had beautiful golden hair but today she yanked at it impatiently.

'Look at my hair. Why can't I have it cut short like everyone else? I hate brushing it every day. Same with all these clothes.' She eyed the blue brocade gown she

15

wore. 'I just want to wear ordinary things sometimes.'

'It sounds as if you don't want to be a princess any more,' the black crow cawed.

She flopped on her bed and heaved a great sigh. 'No, it's not that really, I suppose. It's just, well . . . being a princess all the time. I'd like to do something different. You understand, don't you, Crow?'

Crow nodded. 'Then why don't you? I mean, if you *want* adventure, you can have it. What's to stop you?'

'My parents,' she shot back. 'They won't let me. All they say is, I must behave like a princess – and I'll be happy when I do. Huh!'

She lay in silence for a few moments, then abruptly rolled on to her front and cupped her chin in her hands. She smiled at Crow.

'I tell you what. Why don't we run away from home for a while? You know, like you said once.'

Crow gazed at her intently but said nothing.

'You'd come with me, wouldn't you, Crow? Oh, please say you'll come with me. We could have wonder-ful adventures together, and do all the things you've been telling me about. It'll be so much better than here.

'We'll have to go secretly, of course,' she continued, full of excitement. 'It's the only way. But that will make it even more fun.'

'How will you avoid being recognised?' Crow asked.

'That's no problem. I'll disguise myself as an ordinary girl.'

She rolled off the bed and returned to the mirror. 'I'm quite sure we can find some old clothes in the servants' quarters. And I'll cut my hair,' she said firmly. 'Then nobody will recognise me. What do you think, Crow?'

The bird nodded his head in approval.

'Then you agree? Oh, it'll be marvellous.' She turned eagerly towards him. 'Come on, where shall we go? What shall we do? Will it be far? I don't want to go *too* far.'

Crow suggested they aim for the seaside, which she thought was a marvellous idea. So, for the rest of that afternoon they plotted and planned their great adventure, and it was not until late in the evening that Crow flew noiselessly away into the gathering dusk.

Princess Alena undressed slowly. As she did so, she toyed with the jewel that hung from a slender silver chain around her neck. This was none other than the famed Star Stone of Elmar, so named because of the bright blue living star that burned within its depths. The princess had worn it for as long as she could remember.

The Star Stone was her birth stone – her name meant Star-born – and it made her think of her parents. For a moment she hesitated in her resolve to run away. It seemed as if the stone was gently tugging at her thoughts. But then a determined look came into her eyes.

'No, I will do it. I've always wanted to and now I've made up my mind,' she declared out loud. 'And I don't care!'

With that she prepared for bed.

* * *

Two days later Princess Alena celebrated the arrival of her thirteenth birthday by cutting short her golden hair.

Then she put on the peasant's outfit that she had borrowed from one of the serving maids, having pretended that it was for a dressing-up game. She took a last satisfied glance in the mirror and announced to Crow that she was ready. It was five o'clock in the morning.

Quietly, she opened the lattice window and let down the knotted sheets that she had already tied to the bedpost.

'Make sure the coast is clear, Crow. I don't want to be caught halfway down the wall.'

Crow assured her that all was quiet, so she swung a bag across her shoulder, slipped over the side and slid to the ground.

Keeping close to the house and ducking below the ground-floor windows she crept to a long low hedge that ran to the far garden wall. With a quick glance to the left and right, she darted behind it and crouched her way along its length. An old rowan tree that grew by the wall provided the way out. Swiftly scaling it, she took from her bag a short length of rope that she had brought with her. She tied it to one of the boughs and slithered over the wall and down to the roadway. In a matter of minutes she was clear of the palace. Her hands were chafed but otherwise she was very pleased with herself. Nobody had spotted her so far.

'Well done, Mistress,' whispered Crow. 'That's the most difficult bit over and done with.'

She gave him a cheerful grin.

The streets of the city were quiet at this early hour, with only the occasional noise to force the princess into nervous hiding. As often as not, it proved to be no more than a cat searching for breakfast down an alley.

After nearly half an hour of weaving in and out of the side streets they reached the city gates, just as the watchmen were opening them for the farm labourers to depart for their day's work in the fields.

'This is your chance,' urged Crow. 'Get in among them so you won't be noticed.'

Princess Alena seized her opportunity, and shuffled unnoticed among the crowd of workers and animals that bustled through the gates. Before very long they were alone on the open road.

'There, we've done it!' cried the princess. 'I'm free at last. No more rules and regulations. No more good manners. And no more lessons. I can do what I like from now on. This is what I call a *real* birthday.'

Crow nodded his head energetically. 'Yes, but we mustn't dilly-dally just yet, Mistress. It can't be too long before they discover you are missing and start searching for you.'

'You're right, Crow,' said the princess matter-of-factly. 'But first we must hide this.' She opened her shoulder-bag, revealing the hair that she had cut off.

'I had to bring it all with me,' she explained, 'otherwise somebody might find it and realise I've changed how I look. But now we must get rid of it. Any ideas?'

Crow found a ditch behind a hedgerow and she threw the hair into that. Then she covered it with stones and torn grass. Satisfied with her handiwork, she was ready for the journey.

The road that ran from Elmar to Lin Maril was well used, but a hundred metres or so to the side lay a long stretch of woodland, and they chose this as the more secluded route.

It was one of those warm summer days and the princess felt she hadn't a care in the world. The rich, earthy smell of the woods delighted her and she picked wild flowers and chased squirrels to her heart's content.

'I've not felt so happy in years, Crow. This really was the best idea ever.'

The morning passed quickly and, in spite of the princess's diversions, they made good progress. She ate lunch sprawled in the shade of an old oak tree while Crow perched on a low branch above her, keeping a sharp look-out. Filled with contentment, she snoozed for an hour or so in the hot sun.

It was Crow's gentle nudging that roused her. 'We must be on our way,' he cawed as she stirred.

'Oh, Crow. Why?' she murmured sleepily. 'There's no hurry, is there?'

'No, I suppose not,' he replied. 'But if you want to get to the seaside we'll have to keep moving. I reckon it's all of four days from the city for you to walk it.'

'All right, then.' She smiled as she struggled to her feet. 'I'm coming. Oo! Ouch! I do feel stiff.'

They travelled uneventfully until early evening when they reached the outskirts of Lin Maril, a small but busy town to the south-west of Elmar. The woodland changed to fields, so they rejoined the road; but they had scarcely been on it for more than a few minutes when a clatter of hooves made the princess dart for cover behind a tree. A company of soldiers on horseback, royal guards, flashed by in a cloud of dust.

'They're out looking for me,' she muttered. 'You'd better go spy out the land, Crow.'

The bird flew into the town where, perching unnoticed by an open window, he overheard a soldier's conversation with the mayor. The princess's parents, he learned, had discovered her absence when they entered her room laden with birthday presents at eight o'clock that morning. The alarm was raised and soldiers had been out searching ever since. The King was beside himself with anxiety and the Queen had been in tears for most of the day. Their first thought was that she had been kidnapped, and every house in the city had been searched. However, during the afternoon a sharp-eyed workman had made the awful discovery of the princess's hair in a ditch and since then the search had been extended far and wide.

The whole town was on the alert, so the princess obviously could not spend the night there. Crow returned swiftly and reported his findings to her – but he didn't tell her how upset her parents were.

'Well, I can't stay in Lin Maril, that's for sure,' she said. 'No matter. I'll do what I've always wanted to do. I'm going to sleep under the stars!'

They found a sheltered grassy bank beside a small stream where the princess lay down under the comforting gaze of the moon and, wearied by her journey, soon fell fast asleep.

Crow kept an unblinking watch over her.

3

The Gypsy Caravan

Princess Alena awoke early on the second morning of her escapade, feeling much refreshed. The sun was up and she scrambled down into the nearby brook to wash her grubby face and hands. The cold water made her splash and shout.

'Not so loud, Mistress,' Crow cautioned.

'Oh, don't worry. Nobody's awake yet except me, and I'm so happy,' she cried.

Just then she trod on a sharp stone.

'Ouch! That hurt!'

She hobbled from the stream to find she had cut the ball of her foot.

'Serves me right, I suppose,' she grimaced. 'Still, it doesn't look bad, and we're going to have another fantastic day, aren't we, Crow?'

Crow seemed worried, but she put her sandal on and assured him that she could walk without difficulty.

Breakfast exhausted the food supplies she had brought, but that didn't dampen her spirits in the least.

'We'll live off the land, won't we? I mean, that's what you do, isn't it, Crow? Though I'm not eating the things you like. Ugh!' She made a gesture of disgust at the thought of dining on slugs and worms. 'No, I mean I'll eat fruit and berries. You can tell me which ones are safe. Look, those are blackberries over there, aren't they?'

She hobbled over and tried some. 'Mm, delicious. We'll find lots more on the way, I'm sure.'

It took them about an hour of criss-crossing footpaths to skirt Lin Maril and find their way back onto the little-used road to Anidor. All the while they had to keep themselves hidden from suspicious eyes and many times Crow flew around to make sure the coast was clear. Neither relished the thought of being discovered.

As the morning wore on, Princess Alena's feet began to ache, especially the wounded one, and by lunch time she was limping quite badly. She was also hungry.

'Whew! I'll have to rest a while, Crow,' she called to the hovering bird as she plonked herself on the grassy verge. 'My foot hurts so much. Can you see any food around?'

'Not here,' was the reply.

'Oh, never mind. We'll come across some soon, I expect.'

She struggled to her feet and limped on. But after another half-mile she had had enough. Her spirits were drooping and hunger and thirst were finally taking the glamour off the whole adventure.

'Can't you find food anywhere, Crow?' she cried impatiently.

The bird flew off in a wide circle. He was soon back.

'Good news,' he cawed. 'There's a bit of woodland not far away, with water and plenty of berries.'

'Then take me to it!' she replied with fresh enthusiasm.

Sure enough, Crow led her to a beautiful copse thick with blackberries. The princess ate greedily, but was still hungry – and her foot was now badly swollen.

It was just then that the breeze wafted a delicious

aroma of stew towards her, which set her mouth watering. Intrigued, she followed the smell and came upon a gypsy caravan stationed in a clearing. A man and a woman were cooking their dinner over an open fire. She edged closer.

'Do you think they would know who I am, Crow?' she whispered.

'No, I'm sure they wouldn't recognise you,' he replied. 'Anyway, the gypsies prefer to have as little to do with the soldiers as they can. News won't have reached them yet.'

'Well, what do you think? Shall I ask them for food – and something for my foot?'

'I think you should,' he encouraged.

So the princess hobbled painfully across to the couple, who looked up as a twig cracked beneath her feet.

'Why, hello, missy,' the man called out in a friendly manner. 'This is a surprise. We don't see many folks in these parts. Come and join us. We're just about to have lunch.'

The princess was greatly relieved that they seemed friendly, and delighted at the mention of lunch.

The woman smiled at her. 'You look hungry, m'dear. Come and sit y'self down now. We got rabbit stew and plenty of bread, so help yourself.'

'Oo, thank you,' she replied. 'I really am hungry. It's very kind of you.'

'Think nothing of it,' the woman answered. 'We always offer what hospitality we have to folks that passes through.'

The princess tucked into the meal with relish and the gypsies watched her in amusement.

'You were hungry, weren't you?' said the man. 'Must've been a fair distance y've come.'

'Mmm, all the way from Elmar since yesterday. I . . . I'm on the way to see my uncle at the seaside,' she lied.

That was the first of many untruths she had to tell in answer to their questions over the meal, for Princess Alena discovered that a lie once sown soon produces a harvest of more lies. Feeling bad about it, she made to get up as soon as the meal was over, but her foot caused her to wince.

'Why, you've hurt your foot, m'dear,' said the woman. 'Come into the caravan a moment and I'll see what I can do for it.'

'Well, I've never been inside a real gypsy caravan before,' replied the princess. 'And my foot does hurt. If you don't mind. . . .'

'Of course not. It'll be my pleasure.'

The woman led the way while her husband helped the princess up the steps and through the door. The inside was gloomy and smelt musty. She strained her eyes to see.

'Over here, m'dear,' said the woman.

Princess Alena stumbled against something and, all at once, a small globe began to glow with an unnatural pale light. She gave a start.

'W . . . w . . . what's that?' she stammered.

'Why you're in luck, child,' exclaimed the gypsy woman. 'My crystal ball has something to show you. Take a closer look. Don't be afraid now.'

The princess hesitated. She had been taught from an early age to avoid strange people with magic charms and crystal balls.

'Go on,' urged the woman from behind her. 'It won't hurt you.'

Still she held back.

Exotic shapes passed across the globe. Its light was hypnotic, and strangely attractive. Curiosity tugged at the princess and, believing she could handle matters, she cast aside her doubts and peered into the ball.

At once, a whirring sound filled her ears and her eyes began to sting. She felt giddy and sick. Summoning all her strength she tried to turn away, but found that she was unable to do so. Then something entered her mind like the stab of a knife. She gave a sharp cry and slumped to the floor, unconscious.

A pair of strong hands grasped her limp body and lifted her onto a couch. Two pairs of eyes glowed with evil satisfaction in the gloom.

Crow was already winging his way south-west towards the sea.

* * *

Oswain, ruler of the Great Forest of Alamore, son of Argil and Talesanna, High King and Queen of Elmar and all lands Westwards, donned his travelling cloak and heaved a pack onto his broad shoulders.

'There. Ready to go.' He smiled at those around him but his eyes were serious and already focused on the journey ahead.

'I will accompany you to the ford and the mice will travel as far as you wish. Their task is to relay messages back and forth as necessary.' The speaker was Lord Trotter, King Oswain's chief advisor, a badger of great courage and wisdom who had led the forest folk during the dark years of Hagbane's oppression.[1]

Oswain nodded and turned to the three mice who stood to attention. 'I suggest that we aim for you to be stationed a day's journey apart. Fumble, you will travel with me one day; Mumble, you for two days; Grumble, you for three.'

Each of the mice made to speak but Oswain held up his hand. 'No complaints now. I know you have lived up to your names in the past, but you have much improved. This is a chance to show what you are worth.'

'Yes, sir,' said the three mice in unison as they saluted, even though Fumble did by accident manage to smack Mumble in the eye as he did so.

Trotter raised his eyes heavenwards. 'Good speed and Elmesh go with us all,' he sighed, and with that the company departed, the bright morning sunshine lighting their path through the forest canopy.

The reason for the journey lay in Oswain's dream and in the vision that he had seen in the Star Pool several days ago. Convinced that his young sister, Alena, was in some kind of trouble he had sent word by means of a turtle dove to the palace at Elmar. The city lay a number of days' march west of Alamore and beyond the Cadaelin Mountains. One day later, a hawk brought a message that was short and to the point: 'Urgent. Alena has vanished. She has the Star Stone. Search to the far south-west.'

---

[1] You can read all about this in *Oswain and the Battle for Alamore*.

Oswain was a little puzzled at the appearance of a sparrowhawk, since the palace normally used turtle doves for carrying messages, but he knew that there was no time to lose. His sister was nine years younger than he and although they had not been close, he cared much about her well-being. His dream told him, too, that her disappearance had something to do with the Star Stone. Did she realise its importance? He had to find her, and quickly.

After leaving Trotter at the ford, Oswain and the three mice began their south-westerly trek, knowing neither where it would lead them nor what would happen. Oswain lifted his eyes to the distant mountains. Finding a lost princess in this vast wilderness would be like searching for a needle in a haystack, he thought. He just hoped that the palace had pointed them in the right direction.

* * *

Princess Alena's head felt fit to burst. She winced at the never-ending clatter of saucepans and crockery that accompanied the caravan's jolting, jangling journey along the bumpy roads.

Time passed like a bad dream in the gloom of her mobile prison; she had no idea how long she had lain unconscious nor whether it was night or day. All she knew was that her head hurt and she was desperately thirsty – and she could not move.

In fact, almost eight hours had passed since her capture, and during that time her kidnappers had covered much ground, mostly by means of little-known byways. Their direction lay always towards the sea.

The princess tested her bonds once more, but nothing gave. Her wrists and ankles were firmly tied together by loops of rope running beneath the couch. There seemed no way of escape.

Her thoughts turned again to what had happened. What a fool she had been! The course of events raced through her mind up to the moment when she had looked into the crystal ball. Then pain gripped her head afresh and her brain seemed filled with frightening jabbering voices. She wondered what had happened to Crow. He was her only hope. Perhaps he was following the caravan. Or maybe he had gone to fetch help from the soldiers.

Her train of thought broke as the caravan rattled to a standstill. She waited with bated breath. At length, the door opened and she screwed her eyes at the sudden light from a lantern. It was night outside. The gypsy man hung up the lamp and then returned carrying a dish and a mug. Alena drew back with apprehension.

'Food for you, missy.' He spoke softly but there was no kindness in his eyes.

He loosed her hands and she sat up stiffly, rubbing her wrists.

'No funny business now or else . . . ' he threatened and offered her the mug of water. She drank eagerly and felt instantly better.

'Why have you done this to me?' she demanded, more bravely than she felt. 'You've no right to take me prisoner like this. Let me go at once or else you'll be in real trouble.'

The gypsy laughed. 'Cocky little thing, aren't you? But it won't do you no good. Now, come on, eat this grub 'cos I haven't got all night to waste.'

'I don't want it,' she said sulkily.

'I said, eat it,' retorted the man angrily.

'I won't!'

The gypsy drew back his hand and made to strike. Sullenly, she took the plate and ate the food. He watched her carefully.

'That's better. Do as you're told and no harm'll come to you. Now lie down again.'

The princess, knowing she could do nothing, obeyed and lay sobbing as her wrists were retied and the man withdrew from the caravan. Minutes later they were on the move again.

The journey seemed to last for ever. They stopped twice more – once when, guarded by the woman, she was allowed to go to the toilet, and once more when the man brought her more food. Sometimes she slept for a while, but bad dreams kept waking her. At last they seemed to reach their destination, for the caravan stopped a long while. She could hear the screaming of seagulls.

'Oh, if only I hadn't run away,' she thought miserably. 'I'd have never landed in this mess. What do they want with me? What's going to happen?'

As if in answer to her questions, the door opened with a bang and the gypsy strode in. He released her bonds but held her tightly by the arm as he dragged her up from the couch.

'Come on,' he growled and thrust her towards the

door. 'This is where you get off.'

She stumbled down the steps, wincing with the pain of stiff muscles and because her foot still hurt. Everything was shrouded in mist, except for a vicious-looking sailor who stood before them. She looked in vain for Crow.

'Here she is, then,' said the gypsy.

'And not before time either,' the other answered. 'The Cap'n don't like to be kept waiting, y'know.'

The gypsy spat on the ground. 'I can't help that. We got 'er 'ere as fast as we could. Give us the gold and we'll be on our way.'

The sailor scowled and threw a small leather bag to the gypsy who caught it deftly and thrust the princess forwards at the same time. She stumbled, then caught her balance and made to escape, but the sailor was too quick for her. He grabbed her wrist and pulled her towards him. She struggled and bit his finger hard, an action which, though it earned her a hard cuff round the ear, gave her some small comfort.

With a curse the sailor dragged her off to a small shack and threw her inside. Bolting the door after him he left the princess alone, crying and scared, on the floor.

4

Pirates at The Seagull

'Well, don't just stand there like idiots. Come on,' Peter snapped. He would never admit it but being stuck on the rocks in fog and with the sea rising made him feel very edgy.

Sarah and Andrew said nothing but set off scrambling across the rocks, keeping as close to the cliff wall as they could. Andrew went in front. Suddenly he gave a shout.

'Hey, you two. I think I've found it. Look.'

His brother and sister caught him up. They were expecting to see the beach but instead he was pointing through the mist to a hole in the cliff face.

'It's the tunnel,' cried Sarah. 'Thank goodness for that.'

'Are you sure?' Peter said. 'I thought it was somewhere back there.'

'So did I,' she replied. 'But I suppose we just lost our direction in the fog, don't you?'

'Maybe. Oh well, at least we're safe now,' he answered. 'Go on, then. You found it, Andrew. It might not be so foggy when we reach the top of the cliff.'

Led by Andrew, the three children reached the entrance and began to grope in single file along the tunnel. The mist was so dense that it was impossible to see the other end. In fact, it was billowing towards them like a cloud of white smoke and in a matter of seconds they had completely lost sight even of one another. It was very odd and a bit scary, like the beginning of a weird dream.

Andrew stumbled blindly forwards. He thought he should have reached the end of the tunnel by now and he began to feel for the wall of the round hole. He never found it; instead, to his amazement, he discovered that he was tramping across a pebbly beach, yet he knew for sure that the beach at Trevone was sandy – quite apart from the fact that the round hole came out on top of a cliff and not at beach level. Feeling thoroughly confused, he turned round to look for his brother and sister. What he saw as they emerged from the fog gave him the shock of his life.

'Hey, w–what's happened to your clothes?' he stammered. 'And . . . and w–where are we?'

Peter and Sarah stopped dead in their tracks. In the thinning mist, all three stared first at each other then at their own selves. Gone were their T-shirts and shorts. Instead, each had on a drab, coarse tunic and breeches, complete with knee-high brown leather boots.

Sarah's head swirled and she suddenly felt faint. She grabbed Peter's shoulder for support. 'Oh no! Do you think it's happened again?' she gasped.

Her brother nodded. 'I thought something odd was going on when the mist came in like that. We must be back in Caris Meriac, I reckon.'

'The Land Beyond the Far Places,' Sarah whispered.

'Oh, wow! Brilliant!' exclaimed Andrew.

'Don't say we're going to meet another Hagbane,' wailed Sarah. 'I couldn't stand that. Why've we been sent? Where are we? I don't think I want to be here.'

'Oh, don't start,' said Andrew. 'It was all right last time – in the end. And we'll probably meet all our old friends. I bet it's a reunion party or something.'

'There's only one way to find out,' said Peter, 'and that's to take a look around. Come on, let's get off this beach for starters. But keep your eyes open for trouble.'

The others nodded and they began to tramp up the beach. Eventually they could make out the dim outline of trees through the mist and they made for these, thinking that it might be a part of the Great Forest of Alamore where they knew they had friends.

Instead, they came across an old inn whose faded creaky sign proclaimed it to be The Seagull.

'I think we'd better be careful,' Peter cautioned. 'It doesn't look a very decent place to me. You keep watch and I'll take a snoop round.'

Creeping around the side of the low stone building, he found himself beneath an open window. Cautiously, he peered into the gloomy, smoke-laden bar room. It was crowded with unsavoury looking seafarers who looked as though they had stepped straight out of a history book, but what made him duck down smartly was the fact that two of them were sitting deep in conversation right by the open window. Peter could hear every word they were saying.

'So, y've got the princess, 'ave yer, Jed?'

'Aye, Cap'n Gaspar, sir. That I 'ave. Locked in the outhouse she is. Pretty little thing she be. But got a temper, too. Fair bit my finger she did.'

The other gave a coarse laugh.

'Never mind that, lad. Long as y've got 'er, 'is Eminence'll be right pleased. He'll soon sort 'er temper out and no mistake!'

'Aye, sir, that 'e will. Tell truth, 'e scares me somethin' awful.'

The captain grunted. 'But 'e pays well, Jed, lad. That's what matters. So, soon as I've supped me ale, we'll be off with 'er. Round up the crew, lad. We're in fer a fine reward for today's work.'

Peter had heard enough – was this why they'd been transported here? He hurried back to his brother and sister and quickly recounted what he had over-heard.

'Then we must rescue her at once,' exclaimed Sarah. 'Where's this outhouse or whatever it is? Come on!'

'Hm, maybe. But let's be careful. They look very nasty types to me and we don't want to get caught.'

Sarah gave her brother a look that said, 'Don't be so pathetic!'

He shrugged his shoulders and said, 'OK, then.'

In truth, rescuing a princess from pirates wasn't Peter's idea of fun. It sounded too much like soppy fairy stories. He just hoped he wasn't expected to kiss her! *Yeuk!* So it was with some reluctance that he set off after his brother and sister.

The mist was thickening again, and it took them some time to find their way about, but at last they spotted the dim outline of a small building. They were just about to creep up to it when a shrill scream pierced the mist, followed by some muffled noises.

'It must be the princess,' Sarah cried. 'Come on!'

The three children raced across to the outhouse, but they were too late. The door hung open and the place was empty.

'Which way did they go, d'you think?' Andrew panted.

'Well, I suppose it must be towards the sea, so we'd better follow that path down to the beach,' suggested Peter. He pointed to a narrow track through the grass.

They stumbled along it, though by now the mist was so thick that they could scarcely see in front of their noses. Soon, they came to a point where three paths crossed.

'Now what do we do?' groaned Andrew. 'They could have gone anywhere.'

Peter shrugged his shoulders. 'Haven't a clue,' he said.

'I wish someone sensible was here to help us,' said Sarah, irritated by Peter's attitude. She turned away from her brothers and wandered a short distance into the mist to be by herself.

Just then she heard the fluttering of wings and the next moment a bird landed on her left shoulder, causing her to yelp with surprise. Its plumage was unmistakable, as was its call, *urrr-turrr-turrr*.

'Hello bird. You're a turtle dove, aren't you?' Sarah breathed, not wishing to frighten the bird away. She held out the back of a crooked finger and the bird hopped onto it, but the next instant it began to topple and she had to reach out with her other hand to steady it.

'Poor thing. Are you hurt?' she asked. 'Look at you, all bedraggled and . . . and . . . you are hurt. There's blood on your feathers.'

Then to her amazement, the bird spoke. '*Turrr* it would be a long story *turrr* I was attacked by a hawk *turrr* I just about escaped with my life *urrr* saved by the mist *turr* I cannot deliver my message.'

Only then did Sarah notice the scroll affixed to the bird's leg. 'What shall I do?' she asked.

'*Turrr* take it. You must help *urrr*.'

Sarah carefully lowered the dove to the ground and then removed the tiny scroll. It read: 'The princess has vanished. She has the Star Stone. Go west. Suspect the Island of Zarcos.'

'This is amazing,' she breathed. 'My brother's just heard about a girl being kidnapped. Maybe it's the same person. We were trying to find her but we've lost the way in this fog.'

'*Urrr-turrr* pluck three of my tail feathers *turrr* they are all I can spare but they will help you when you need them *turrr* but you may use each one only once.'

'Won't it hurt you?' Sarah whispered.

'*Turrr* not if you believe. I have come from Queen Talesanna *urrr-turrr-turrr*.'

At the mention of Oswain's mother, Sarah's heart leapt. She carefully plucked three fine feathers from the turtle dove's tail. To her immense relief they came away easily and the dove seemed not to be harmed.

'What about you?' she asked.

'*Urrr* I must rest. Put the message back on my leg and leave me in the hands of Elmesh *urrr* we will see *turrr-urrr-turrr-turrr*.'

Sarah knew now what to do. She replaced the message, tucked the feathers into her jerkin and then quickly found her way back to where her brothers still stood looking lost.

'Where have you been?' Peter demanded.

'I bet she's been to the loo,' Andrew piped up.

'Of all the times . . .' Peter began.

'No I haven't,' Sarah interrupted. 'I'll explain later, but come on. We've got to catch up with those pirates. This is the path.'

She pointed to the left and started off at once, leaving her brothers speechless to follow her.

It wasn't long before they were in sight of the beach. The mist was more patchy here and they could see a longboat floating close to land with the oarsmen at the ready. Two men on the shore were holding someone who, in spite of her clothes, they took to be the princess. A number of barrels and boxes stood nearby awaiting stowage. The children took their chance, and hoping that nobody would see them, they crept through the mist until they were hiding right behind the pile of cargo.

'Now what do we do?' whispered Andrew. 'We can hardly take that lot on – not unless someone's got hand grenades and a rocket launcher.'

Peter rolled his eyes. 'Don't be stupid,' he whispered. 'This is serious.' He thought for a moment. 'Maybe we should create a diversion or something.'

'Whatever we do, we'll have to be quick. Look, the boat's landing,' said Sarah. 'They'll have her aboard in next to no time.'

The children's problem was resolved for them sooner than they expected. Without any warning, three pairs of rough hands seized them from behind and dragged them to their feet. Sarah screamed and the boys yelled with surprise. Each one struggled to break free, but it was no good; they were well and truly caught.

From where she stood in the grip of her own captors Princess Alena turned her head to see what the rumpus was about. To her surprise she saw three children being dragged across the beach and she wondered whether they were from royal families as well.

However, before she could think further, a man came swaggering out of the patchy mist dressed in a dilapidated captain's uniform and carrying a walking stick. He strode up to the princess.

'Well, well, what 'ave we here?' He addressed the princess with mock politeness. 'A princess! Allow me to introduce m'self, your majesty. Cap'n Gaspar's the name and I be at your service, ma'am.' He grinned through broken yellowed teeth. 'I request the pleasure of your company aboard me ship.'

5

On Board Grimwolf

Princess Alena turned her head away from the captain. 'I do not accept your offer,' she said haughtily.

He gave a disdainful sniff. 'Have it your own way, then. But you're coming, whether you like it or not!' He turned to Peter, Sarah and Andrew with a gleam in his eye. 'And who might you be, may I ask? You friends of 'ers?'

'Found 'em spying, Cap'n,' explained one of their captors, a swarthy sailor wearing a leather jerkin and a black headband.

'Spyin', eh? Fifty lashes each from the yardarm for that, I reckon. What've yer got to say fer y'selves?'

The children stood in stubborn silence.

'Well, we'll loosen your tongues later. And if we don't, 'is Eminence certainly will. Tide won't wait for us now. Take 'em aboard, men.'

With that, the princess and the children were frog-marched to the water's edge where they were bundled into the longboat.

Peter peered over the prow as the boat bobbed through the breakers and into open water. Through the mist, he could make out a full-masted galleon riding at anchor in the swell. In spite of their danger, he felt a thrill at the thought of being taken aboard what must be a real pirate ship. Andrew joined him.

'Wow, look at that! Can you see what she's called?'

'No, not yet. It's still too misty.'

They hadn't long to wait, for with much creaking of oars and grunting by the sailors the boat soon drew close enough to make out the rigging and the name of the ship quite clearly. Painted in blood-red letters on the prow was the single word *Grimwolf*. The figurehead beneath the bowsprit reflected the name – a ghastly wolf's head with blood dripping from its fangs.

Once alongside, the sailors quickly transferred their captives to the ship and threw them into a cabin beneath the forecastle. Almost immediately the sails were unfurled, the anchor hoisted and with a creaking of timbers *Grimwolf* was under way.

'Well, here we are,' said Andrew. 'Now what?'

He looked around the cabin. Apart from a table, a jug of water and some piles of straw, there was nothing else in the room. The only light came from a barred window set in the door. It would not be a comfortable trip, he thought.

'We'd better introduce ourselves,' Sarah whispered to her brothers.

Peter addressed the princess. 'Hello. I'm Peter, and this is my sister Sarah and my brother Andrew.'

'I'm Alena,' she replied sullenly from the corner.

'Hello,' said the other two.

Sarah sat down beside the princess. 'You're a princess, aren't you? We overheard the pirates speaking, or at least Peter did.'

She nodded glumly. 'A lot of good it's doing me now, isn't it?'

'Why have they kidnapped you?' Andrew asked. 'Is it

for a ransom or something?'

'I suppose so,' she answered. 'But I can't understand how they knew who I was. Nobody followed us. No one even knew.'

Prodded by their questions, she proceeded to tell them all that had happened since leaving the palace.

'You shouldn't really have run away, should you?' said Peter when she was through.

'That's my business,' she snapped. 'I'm a princess so I can do as I please. How was I to know this was going to happen to me? And what's happened to Crow? And . . . and where are they taking me? They have no right . . .' A stab of pain shot through her head, which made her wince and then she burst into tears.

Sarah put her arms around the princess. 'Don't worry, Alena. We'll get out of it somehow. I just know we will.' There was more conviction in her words than in her heart.

Before they could say more the cabin door crashed open and in strode Captain Gaspar with his henchman, Jed. The children retreated into the corner, but Jed grabbed Peter and dragged him before the captain. Addressing him roughly, the captain demanded, 'Now then, laddie, I'll not take nonsense from you. What were you doing spyin' on us? Answer me now, or Jed's liable to get a bit rough with a rope's end. What's yer business?'

Peter remained silent. The captain nodded to Jed who immediately twisted the boy's arm behind his back causing him to cry out in pain.

Sarah hurled herself at the pirate. 'Leave him alone, you rotten bully!' she cried. 'I'll tell you what happened.'

Captain Gaspar motioned Jed to let Peter go. 'Well, a real spitfire and no mistake,' he grinned through his dirty teeth. 'I like a wench with a bit o' spirit. So, let's hear you now.'

'We're here 'cos we arrived on the beach and got lost in the mist. So we found our way to The Seagull, and that's where we overheard your evil plan. We decided to try and rescue the princess. And I think you're very horrible people,' she finished breathlessly.

Captain Gaspar roared with laughter. 'So that's it, is it? Well, you silly brats, you've got y'selves into a lot of trouble, 'aven't you? 'Cos you're going to 'ave to come along with the princess now. 'Is Eminence will sort out what to do with you. But I don't fancy yer chances much.' He motioned to Jed. 'Come on. We'll leave 'em to stew. Teach 'em to meddle in things that be none of their business.'

With that the two pirates left, locking the door behind them and leaving the children to their own devices.

'Is it really true what you said?' asked Princess Alena.

'Well, yes, it is really,' Sarah replied, wondering how she could explain about the round hole. She thought it better that the pirates didn't know about that.

Princess Alena gave a watery smile. She spoke in a friendly way now. 'Well, thank you for trying. I'm only sorry I've got you into all this. Goodness knows what will happen now.'

For a while they sat in brooding silence.

'Hey,' cried Andrew suddenly. 'What city did you say you came from?'

'Elmar,' replied the princess.

'B . . . b . . . but, isn't that Oswain's city?'

'You know Oswain?'

'Yes,' chorused the children.

She sat in silence for a moment, then said quietly, 'Oswain is my older brother.'

'Of course,' said Sarah. 'And your mother is Queen Talesanna. Now it makes sense.'

Astounded by the news everyone started gabbling at once.

It took them the best part of an hour to recount all their previous adventures. The hardest part was explaining how they had come from another realm and they were far from convinced that the princess fully believed them. She saw very little of Oswain in any case and appeared not to have a very high opinion of him, which Sarah found hard to understand.

Even so, this knowledge greatly cheered them up, and when Jed came in with food and drink during early evening he was taken aback to find his captives laughing and joking together.

That night, as they slept on the piles of straw, Sarah dreamed.

In her dream she was feeling her way through a white cloud. Her outstretched hand searched the mist, though she did not know for what. Moments later, she found herself in a dark cavern piled high with treasure. She walked towards a door that opened of its own accord, and there hung a resplendent gem that entranced her with its silvery-blue beauty.

Then, to her horror, a green claw grasped the stone, snuffing out its light. She wrestled to prevent it happening, but was instantly surrounded by a pack of howling wolves. With a shriek she ran and ran down an endless black tunnel, pursued by the wild creatures. She felt her heart bursting and could go on no farther when a turtle dove flew in front of her and exploded in a cloud of feathers . . . and there her dream ended. She woke to find the silvery morning light was just beginning to penetrate the small window.

It wasn't long before the others woke up and she told them of her dream, but she didn't feel she should say anything about the turtle dove and the feathers. They puzzled over the meaning of the rest of the dream until Andrew suddenly smacked his fist into the palm of his hand.

'Got it!' he cried. 'They're after your jewels. That's what it is.'

'No,' said Sarah softly. 'I think it's just one jewel. Have you got something special, Alena?'

The princess hesitated. Then she drew from her dress the Star Stone. The others gazed in wonder at the jewel. Hardly any outside light reflected off its many faces; instead, a vivid blue star shone with radiant splendour from deep within the crystal clear stone. The star seemed to be suspended in space as though shimmering in a universe all of its own.

'Do you think it's this?' she said.

Awe-struck, Sarah said, 'I'm sure that's what I saw in my . . .'

Just at that moment there was a sound outside and the door began to open.

'Quick, put it away!' urged Peter.

Jed walked in. 'On yer feet,' he commanded. 'No, not you.' He motioned to the princess. 'Only these three. Come on, outside. There's work for the likes of you.'

Reluctantly they left the cabin. For the rest of the morning they were kept busy scrubbing decks and coiling ropes, so that they didn't see the princess again until a cry of 'Land ho!' from the crow's nest told them their journey was at an end.

Coming rapidly into view was a small island not far from the mainland, although to the south of where the children had been captured. Before long sailors were scrambling up the rigging and reefing in the sails to the commands of the captain and his bosun. The children watched as the vessel drew alongside an empty stone quay and made fast.

The gangplank dropped with a clatter and a few moments later a sailor dragged Princess Alena from her cabin to join the others.

'Come on,' snarled Jed. 'Off yer get.' He pushed all four down the plank and onto the quay side. Captain Gaspar followed.

Just then, a door opened in a small keep at the end of the quay, and before the children's frightened eyes there emerged a grotesque green goblin. Behind him followed a pack of slavering grey wolves.

Sarah screamed. Her dream seemed about to come true.

6

The Grey Tower

Gublak was horribly fat, a monstrosity of squat green flab with sharply pointed ears and cold, calculating eyes that glinted like emeralds. His bald head glistened in the sun, as did the gold chains that hung from his bulging neck and decorated the black caftan that he wore.

Time seemed to stand still as he approached the small group on the quay side. An oppressive silence hung over everything. No sailor dared venture down the gangplank to join Captain Gaspar, for they lived in dread of the goblin.

'So, you have arrived,' Gublak addressed the captain in a husky voice that carried a barely hidden menace. He looked first to Sarah and then to Alena. 'Which of these is the princess? Who are these others?' he demanded.

'If it pleases your Eminence, this one is Princess Alena,' the captain answered with respect. 'These other three we caught spyin'. Brought 'em along for your wisdom to judge. Or shall I 'ave 'em killed now, sir?'

'No, fool. I shall see what they are worth first.' He gave an oily smile. 'You have done well, Captain. Better than I expected.'

He reached into his caftan and drew out a large ruby which he tossed to the captain. 'A bonus for you, my friend. The gold you will find in the keep when I have departed. I know your miserable crew will not dare come ashore until then.'

'Your Eminence is most kind,' replied Captain Gaspar as he leered over the ruby in his grubby palm.

Gublak turned to his wolves and addressed the leader of the pack. 'Take them away, Ulris. These three to the kitchens, and the princess – take her to the Grey Tower.'

Ulris snarled and bared his fangs. 'At your bidding, Eminence.'

He fixed his baleful yellow eyes on the captives and, filled with fear, they had no option but to obey. Surrounded by the wolves, they stumbled off along the quay while the goblin followed at his own leisurely pace.

Gublak's fortress stood on the summit of the island at the head of a long winding track. It looked grey and forbidding, with tall towers and stern turrets frowning over the forest. The trees stretched away in all directions from the rocky outcrop upon which the fortress stood. The stench of wolves was everywhere and the children's hearts sank as they passed under the gloomy archway that led into the main courtyard. Here they were split up.

'Don't be scared,' Peter shouted to Princess Alena as she was led away. 'We'll think of something, don't you worry.'

She turned and gave him a watery smile. The brief warmth of their companionship made her loneliness feel all the more bitter.

Peter, Sarah and Andrew were immediately put to work in the basement kitchens where piles of unwashed dishes and sacks of vegetables awaited their attention.

Lizard-like guards with long tails and scaly skin

watched over them as they toiled. They later found out that these were called Urgils. Each guard carried a sword, the flat of which was used across the children's shoulders whenever they slacked at their labours or attempted to speak to one another.

They slaved like this all afternoon, and it was not until late evening that they were allowed any food. By the time they were thrown into a dungeon for the night all three felt ready to drop.

'Whew! I'm exhausted,' said Andrew as they flopped down.

'Me too,' agreed Sarah. 'What a day. I thought it would never come to an end. I've never seen so much washing up.'

'And don't forget all we did this morning on the ship,' added Andrew. He rolled over to face his brother. 'What are we going to do, Pete?'

'I don't know,' he replied. 'I don't fancy being a slave much longer, that's for sure. I mean, what kind of revolting creature is that? What with those guards and wolves as well. Goodness knows what they've done with Alena. We've just got to find a way to get out of here.'

'I do hope she's all right,' said Sarah. 'Do you think it's really that jewel he's after?'

'Can't think what else it can be, can you?' said Peter.

'Then why didn't someone just kill Alena, or at least knock her out, and steal it?' Andrew queried. 'Surely that would've been the easy way?'

'Perhaps it's not as simple as that,' replied his brother.

* * *

Princess Alena, meanwhile, was seated in a large room at the top of a high tower. She was completely alone and the door was locked.

To her surprise, her prison was comfortably furnished with all that was needed to make her feel at home, and plenty of food had been provided for her to eat. After some initial suspicions that it might be poisoned, she had hungrily eaten it all.

Even more astonishing were the elegant clothes that she found in the wardrobe. They were all her size and of even better quality than she was used to wearing back home. She tried some on and was particularly taken with a silvery-white gown that she decided to wear for a while. Perhaps this adventure was going to turn out all right after all. At least she was being treated as a princess should be.

Then her mind went back to her newly found friends. Whatever would become of them? Nor could she forget that she was a prisoner herself – however nice the room might be. She paced to and fro across the floor.

'Why doesn't anyone come for me?' she muttered. 'What does that ugly creature want, anyway?'

She felt the Star Stone around her neck. 'Well, he's not having this, that's for sure. It belongs to me and me alone. So there!'

She gazed out of the windows. The view was stunning. Not only could she see the courtyards and battlements of the castle below, but the whole expanse of the forested island and the blue sea beyond. In one direction she could make out the hazy outline of a mountainous coastline. She wondered where it was.

At long last, as the sun was setting and an ominous

green mist was rising from the trees, there came the sudden rattle of a key in the door. She sat on the bed gripping the covers tightly as the door opened. One of the Urgils entered.

'His Eminence requires your presence at his table,' he said briefly. 'You are to accompany me now.'

Knowing it was pointless to argue, and curious to discover what was to happen, Princess Alena allowed herself to be escorted down the stairs. They passed along many corridors lit with burning torches until they reached a pair of large doors flanked by two guards. At a sign from her escort the doors were swung open and she was ushered into a spacious hall.

Before her stood Gublak, and beyond she could see a table heavily laden with food. A fire burned brightly upon a massive hearth, casting flickering shadows around the walls.

'Ah, welcome, Princess Alena. Welcome to Zarcos.' His voice possessed a silky huskiness, but she knew it concealed malice. There could be no mistaking those eyes. 'I see you have found garments more becoming for a princess. I trust they are to your liking. Won't you please join me for dinner?'

'I don't know who you are,' she replied coldly, 'but I've been kidnapped, maltreated, and brought here without any explanation whatsoever. I am extremely cross and require you to release both myself and my companions this very instant.'

Her face grew very red and she clenched her fists angrily.

'Forgive me, dear Princess. I will explain everything. First, however, let me introduce myself. My name is

Gublak, and I am the ruler of this island. You will have realised by now that my power also extends far beyond its shores.

'As to the reason I have brought you here – you have something that I want, something I dearly desire.' His eyes glittered with unconcealed greed and she shrank back with distaste. 'You see,' he went on, 'I am a collector of beautiful things. I have amassed treasures more than you can imagine, vast caverns of gold, silver and jewels. Works of art that would dazzle you. These bring me great satisfaction – but, alas, beautiful as they are, they are lifeless. There is no *real* power in gold.

'But *you* have something more,' he continued. 'You possess the Star Stone of Elmar. That is what I most desire.'

'The Star Stone is mine,' she replied in a steady voice, though her heart was thumping hard. 'I am not prepared to give it up.'

Gublak smirked. 'We shall see. I am very rich and am prepared to pay a great price for this jewel. You could be a very wealthy princess, and wield great power with the treasures I would bestow upon you for this . . . this trinket. It could be all yours to do with as you pleased. Just think of it.'

'The Star Stone is not for sale,' she replied shortly. 'That's all there is to it. Now let me go back to my room while you plan how you are going to return me to the mainland.'

The goblin glared at her determined face. 'Very well. For the moment, that is how I shall leave it. But first, there is something I must put to the test. Guards!'

The two Urgils rushed in.

'You, seize her,' he commanded one of them.

Before the princess could move, her arms were firmly pinioned behind her back. Gublak spoke to the other guard.

'Remove the jewel that hangs about her neck.'

Princess Alena fought vainly, lashing out with her feet as the scaly creature approached. His claw took hold of the chain and he lifted the jewel from her dress. Yet the moment he laid his hand upon the Star Stone itself, a sigh like an endless sadness escaped his jaws, and at once he fell dead at her feet.

The other guard released her with a start and sprang back, while the princess stared horror-struck at the fallen creature.

'Then the rumour is true,' muttered Gublak. 'No matter, no matter.' To the remaining Urgil he ordered, 'Return the princess to the tower and lock her in securely.'

Princess Alena sat in bed an hour later with a certain satisfaction in her heart. She fingered the Star Stone with an affection that she had never felt before.

'Hm,' she thought. 'He won't try that again in a hurry. I feel sorry about the guard, but that's not really my fault. Perhaps there's more power in the Stone than I thought. Maybe things will turn out all right after all.'

With that she lay down to sleep.

Yet it was not to be a pleasant night for Princess Alena. The moment her head touched the pillow it began to throb. Her mind was filled with the image of the crystal ball in the gypsy caravan and try as she might she could not shut it out. Weird voices began to jabber again. She broke into a cold sweat and tossed and turned in her bed. A cool wind whistled through the windows, blowing the curtains into wildly contorted shadows. Things fell. The room span. At times she thought there were people walking around. She heard strange scurrying noises and couldn't tell whether they were in her head or under the bed. She felt terribly afraid.

Then the wolves began their blood-chilling howls from far below. Shivering, she clutched at the bedclothes and wished for the dawn.

In his room Gublak smiled grimly as he sat, fingertips touching beneath his chin. 'Stubborn she may be, but we will see what a night in the Grey Tower will do about that!' he mused to himself.

7

Trouble in Moonwood

Oswain and the three mice travelled steadily south-west across the Waste Plains. Soon, they had left the Great Forest and the River Wendle far behind.

Fumble, Mumble and Grumble often lived up to their names but they had proved to be very brave in the past. Like all animals in the Great Forest they were larger than life, so they had little difficulty keeping up with Oswain's powerful strides. For all that, they were relieved when the first day's march ended.

'Ow, my poor paws ache,' groaned Fumble. He tried to lick his hind left paw but fell over and bit his own tail instead. 'Ouch!' he cried. 'That hurt!'

'Corsidus,' said Mumble. 'Yuhshudlokaforyerbit.'

Grumble muttered something rude about mice that had four left feet and tongues with knots in them. The other two jumped on him and bundled him in the dust, much to Oswain's amusement.

'Ah well, maybe you're not so tired, after all. Perhaps we should carry on for another hour or two,' he suggested.

The mice stopped at once and said that they really were tired and had best be getting some sleep. Whereupon, they curled up together right where they were, leaving Oswain to keep watch until it was dark.

Wrapped in his cloak he gazed across the rolling

moorland. The moon had not yet risen and the stars shone like diamond dust, their magical light kissing with silver the crests of the dark and distant hills. Farther away lay the huge bulk of the southern Cadaelin Mountains, and their snow-capped peaks were tinged as blue as the stars themselves.

Oswain wondered where his sister might be under this vast sky. Had his mother been right to urge him in this direction? He hoped so, but had no way of knowing for sure. He sighed and glanced over to the sleeping mice. It was time to get some sleep himself. 'Elmesh help her,' he prayed as he lay down and pulled his cloak snug around him.

Was it his imagination? He wasn't sure. Just as his eyes were closing he fancied he saw a flash of light on the mountains. For a while he strained his eyes at the dark mass, but then sleep overtook him and he watched no more.

Though he did not know it, the light flashed again while he slept, and again.

* * *

The following day dawned bright and clear. Eager to be off, Oswain jostled the mice awake with the promise of breakfast. As arranged they left Fumble to await further instructions, much to his relief since his feet still ached – and to everyone else's because they wouldn't have to put up with his continual tripping over.

'If we are not back within four days you must go for

help,' Oswain instructed. 'Should we need you sooner, Grumble or Mumble will run back to tell you.'

By lunch time, the mountains were much closer and their crags stood out magnificently in the sunlight. It was around then that they picked up the beginnings of a trail, which surprised them because this part of the land was supposed to be uninhabited. Perhaps Oswain's mother knew something after all and his sister had passed this way – though something told him it wasn't as simple as that.

They decided to follow the track. At first it wound across the moor but towards late afternoon the landscape began to change and the path led them up into a rocky pass surrounded by high buttresses jutting from steep cliffs. It was hot work in the sun and by the time they emerged onto a broad plateau the three companions were exhausted.

'Whew, that will do for today, I think,' gasped Oswain.

Mumble said he was delighted to hear it, but it came out as 'the night has an ear fit', which, as Grumble said, was complete nonsense.

Oswain scanned the late afternoon scene. Far to the east he could see the pink haze beyond which lay the Great Forest of Alamore. He turned south and sniffed the air. It carried a faint tang of the sea but the view was lost in blue haze.

To the north and west, however, it was dark, for the sun had dropped behind the mountains casting a cool shadow over the landscape. Ahead of their path there rose a dark mass of trees.

'Moonwood,' Oswain muttered. 'Well, we'll not

venture there tonight, that's for sure. Let's make camp right here.'

* * *

The next morning, leaving Mumble behind as planned, Oswain and Grumble set off together on their third day's trek. The path took them straight into Moonwood.

'I have heard strange tales of this place,' said Oswain. 'Travellers here – and there have been few – tell of wraiths and of paths that change so that you can go neither forwards nor back but only in circles until you go mad with despair. They say you must leave gold or a precious stone for a night. By morning it will be gone but then your path will be plain once more.'

'It's enough to make your fur bristle,' said Grumble. 'Do we really have to go this way?'

'We've little choice,' Oswain answered. 'There are no other paths and if this does lead to Alena then we must follow it, whatever happens.'

They had entered an ancient beech wood and although it was summer the ground was still littered with flurries of bronzed leaves that had not yet rotted away. Nothing much else grew and although their track was clear to see, there were no landmarks to guide them.

Oswain and Grumble had been walking for about an hour when their path petered out without warning, leaving them in the middle of nowhere and surrounded by trees whose thick silver-grey trunks all looked the same.

They stopped and looked back the way they had come. To their amazement there was no sign of the path at all – no sign that they had just walked to this point. A chill breeze had sprung up and, in spite of himself, Oswain shivered. Worse, he had the distinct feeling that he and Grumble were being watched.

Grumble grew very alarmed and he began to run in small circles, sniffing the ground for all he was worth.

'Easy now, Grumble,' Oswain urged. 'There's no need to panic.'

'I-I'm not panicking,' Grumble squeaked. 'I'm just terrified. That's all!'

'We must remember the first rule about being lost,' Oswain said.

'W-what's that?'

'Stop, sit down, and think,' he replied.

Grumble calmed down and they began to plan their next move.

'I don't believe all that nonsense about wraiths and disappearing paths,' said Oswain. 'We've just lost our bearings – nothing more.'

'If you say so,' said Grumble, who was far from convinced.

'All we need do is find the path we've lost, set our bearings and then discover where it starts up again ahead of us.'

'How do we do that?'

'It's easy,' Oswain replied. 'I'll stand here so you can see me while you begin to track out in a spiral; you know, wider and wider circles, until you find the path – but keep me in sight.'

Grumble did as Oswain suggested and sure enough

he found the path they had travelled a hundred or so metres to the right of where Oswain stood.

Oswain ran to join him. 'Good. Well done. Now for the next part,' he explained. 'You start zigzagging forwards until you find the next section of the path. But keep checking on where I'm standing.'

'How come I get to do all the running about?' Grumble complained.

'Because if I did it you would be invisible to me. Your fur is almost the same colour as that of the trees, but if you do it you'll be able to see me.'

'Huh!'

That settled, Grumble set off. Watched by Oswain, he ran hither and thither among the trees, getting farther and farther away all the time.

'Not too far, Grumble,' Oswain called. 'I'll come to you and then we'll try again.'

There was no reply. Instead, Oswain heard a sharp hiss followed by a faint cry.

'Grumble, what is it?' Oswain cried, but there was no answer save for the uneasy rustle of the wind in the trees.

Ignoring his own advice, Oswain ran forward to where he thought he had last seen Grumble, calling the mouse's name as he went. Yet, however hard he looked and however hard he listened he could find no trace of his companion – and by then he had completely lost track of where he was himself.

All day he searched, and by late afternoon he was nearing despair. The lengthening shadows told him that darkness would fall early in Moonwood, it being so close to the nearby mountains.

The thought gave him an idea. If Grumble was dead there was little that he could do except grieve. If, however, he was still alive and had been captured then it was likely that his captors had taken him to a place of hiding on the far side of the woods, near the mountains. Grim-faced, he began to follow the shadows and walk into the gathering gloom.

Throughout all this time he had felt eyes upon him, mocking his hopeless task. Now the thought angered him. If whoever watched could hide themselves then so could Oswain – the King of the Great Forest of Alamore was, after all, no stranger to woodlands!

He waited until it was quite dark and then slipped behind a great beech, pulling his hood over his head as he did so. Then he began to wait.

All was quiet. He strained his eyes into the gloom. Then he saw it – a faint shadow flitted between the trees ahead. Moving with caution from tree to tree, Oswain began to follow. The tales of wraiths came back to him but he began to see that this particular wraith was searching for him but all the time moving in a definite direction – hardly the behaviour of a ghost! Oswain smiled grimly.

Gradually the woods began to thin and he realised that they were nearing the foothills of the mountains. The ground grew stony under foot. Then he spied his quarry; it was a definite man shape, but very short and limping, too.

Puzzled, Oswain followed, moving as silent as a wraith himself. He saw the man limp towards the base of a tree that grew next to a rocky outcrop. With a glance over his shoulder, the figure lifted a latch and a door swung open. Noiselessly, he vanished inside and the door closed. Moments later, Oswain was beside the door. The faint glow of a lamp shone through a crack and he could hear the sounds of movement inside.

Oswain decided to wait. To charge into the unknown was to invite trouble, so he squatted beside the door and let his thoughts turn towards Grumble.

'If you're still alive, my friend, do not lose heart,' he willed. 'I shall find you.'

After about an hour, Oswain's patience was rewarded. From the far distant mountains northwards he saw the faint glint of a light. So he hadn't been mistaken the other night. A movement inside made him duck into the shadows. The next instant the door opened and the occupant limped outside carrying an oil lamp. Oswain watched as the stocky little man signalled a reply, covering and uncovering the lamp with a piece of cloth. Answering flashes came from the mountain.

At length the signalling ceased and the figure turned towards the door. Oswain sized him up – squat and broad, his features were unmistakably those of a Dweorg. Oswain leapt upon him and threw him to the ground, dousing the lamp in the process. He knew that Dweorgs were immensely strong and this one was no exception. He flung Oswain from him as though he were a baby. Oswain leapt in again as the figure struggled for the door of his lair.

It was a hard tussle but eventually Oswain had the better of him and pinned him face down on the ground.

'Now, who are you and what have you done with my companion?' he growled.

The Dweorg cursed and spat but at last gave in.

'I am Brankleshanks,' he said. 'And I bid you little welcome, Oswain of Alamore.'

* * *

Oswain sat on a hard wooden chair in the Dweorg's den. After overpowering him, Oswain had forced the Dweorg indoors and demanded to know the where-abouts of Grumble.

Insisting first that Oswain release him and behave like a proper guest in the Dweorg's home, Brankleshanks had seated himself in an old armchair and lit a long clay pipe. Puffing on the stem, he began to tell his story – a strange tale, though not all of it would prove to be the truth.

'I am, as you can see, a Dweorg, and like all my race nothing pleases me more than to delve the roots of the world in search of fine jewels and precious metals. By the sweat of my brow I amassed a goodly hoard, as wor-thy as the labours of any of my ancestors.'

Oswain looked him over, noting the clean-shaven fleshy features, the deep, dark eyes and his stern fur-rowed forehead. Brankleshanks wore a leather jerkin over a coarse grey tunic girt with a wide belt. In the cor-ner of the hearth lay a crossbow and an axe. Oswain would keep an eye on these and on the large knife that Brankleshanks carried in his belt.

'I have met Dweorgs in Elmar,' said Oswain. 'Many of the palace treasures owe their origin to the labours of your people and you are held in high regard.'

The Dweorg nodded. 'So we should be,' he said. 'Mining is hard work and dangerous. The darkness does not easily yield its bright secrets to the light.' He paused and relit his pipe. 'All this continued for many a year until one day I had a visit – a goblin named Gublak turned up one May morning with an extraordinary offer. He would give me one precious stone for all the gold, silver and gems that I possessed.'

'It would have to be a most exceptional jewel,' said Oswain.

The Dweorg flashed him a glance. 'It was. It was. He offered me nothing less than a Star Stone.'

At this Oswain gave a start. 'A Star Stone. Which one? Whose?' he demanded.

'Nobody's,' Brankleshanks replied shortly. 'What he showed me looked like a Star Stone, at least I thought so, for I had never actually set eyes on one myself. All I knew was that such gems were almost transparent and that they contained a living star. The one he showed me appeared to fit the description.' The Dweorg frowned. 'Like a fool I took it in exchange for all my wealth. I even signalled the news to my brother, Dringol, who works the northern range.'

'What happened?' Oswain asked.

'One day later the light died in the Star so that it remained no more than a blue dot. You can imagine my feelings. All I had laboured for was gone. I decided to go after the goblin at once.'

'Did you find him?'

'I did, or rather, he found me. I walked into an ambush. I suppose he knew that I would come after him once the truth was out. I knew then, of course, that this was no misfortune but a deliberate lie, so I demanded the return of my wealth. He refused to my face and told me to go dig for some more.'

Oswain looked around the Dweorg's home. It was built of simple wood and stone. A small fire smouldered on the smoke-blackened hearth and a few rustic tools hung from the dusty rafters. The furniture consisted of no more than a dresser and a table, the chair upon which Oswain sat and the Dweorg's armchair. If Brankleshanks had made further wealth there was little to show for it here.

The Dweorg noted his observations. 'This is all there is,' he said. 'I am no longer able to mine the mountains. When Gublak mocked me I became angry and drew my axe. However, before I could use it, wolves darted from the undergrowth and attacked me. I killed some but I was soon overpowered. Then Gublak ordered one, Ulris the pack leader, cruelly to bite my leg so that I was crippled for life.'

Oswain winced. 'The pain must have been terrible,' he said.

'It was. They left me bleeding and badly injured.' He laid aside his pipe and stared deeply into the fire. 'Well did my mother prophesy when she named me: brankled I am in my shanks!'

'It is an evil tale,' said Oswain. 'You have suffered a great injustice at the hands of this goblin.'

'True. But I have vowed my revenge,' the Dweorg answered, turning to face him. 'And with your help I shall have it. I shall kill the goblin and regain what is mine.'

'I don't see how I can help you,' said Oswain looking

perplexed. 'I am on a quest to find my lost sister and I must also find out what has happened to my travelling companion.'

The Dweorg's eyes gleamed. 'That is why you will assist me, Oswain of Alamore.'

'What do you mean?'

'I know the whereabouts of your sister and of your companion.'

'Then you will tell me, and tell me quickly,' Oswain insisted, half rising to his feet and feeling he had wasted enough time already.

'Gublak has your sister. I should not have cared, except that I saw a way to avenge my own wrongs. You see, I cannot walk very far, and certainly not through the mountains. But you are strong enough to carry me. I will take you to your sister and I shall slay the goblin. So we both shall have our reward.'

Oswain gave the Dweorg a guarded look. 'Your injuries I can see and I have no reason to disbelieve your story, but how can I know that you are telling the truth about Alena? Nor have you mentioned the fate of Grumble, my travelling companion. You know more than you are saying and, I believe, were watching me as I searched for him. What have you done with Grumble?'

The Dweorg picked up his pipe and calmly set to puffing it once again. 'If Grumble is a mouse then you should know that he is well ahead of you,' – here the Dweorg chuckled – 'and he thinks that you are well ahead of him!'

Oswain was angry. 'Why then did you let us both spend a whole precious day searching for one another? My sister is in deadly danger if what you say is true of this Gublak.'

The Dweorg's thick lips twisted into a smile. 'A mouse cannot carry me. It is your help I need, Oswain, and I wasn't going to lose such a chance. When you thought that you would hide from me and reverse the roles of watcher and watched, I simply played your game and lured you to my house. By then your mouse was well on his way into the mountains.'

Oswain's eyes narrowed suspiciously. 'You could have asked me to carry you and still have had Grumble with me.'

'I don't like mice.'

'And I don't like liars.'

'That is fine, so what are you going to do?'

Oswain rose to his feet and paced the room in frustration. 'This will get us nowhere. How do you know that this goblin has my sister?' he demanded.

'That,' said the Dweorg, 'I will tell you in the morning when you agree to take me with you. And now, if you do not mind, I will sleep and I suggest you do the same. It will be a long day tomorrow.'

At last, and after much arguing, reluctantly Oswain had to agree – though he would not sleep easily in the Dweorg's lair.

Meanwhile, not far away in Moonwood and unknown to Oswain, Grumble lay unconscious inside a hollow tree trunk. His leg was bound to an iron ring with a stout cord and an arrow pierced his left ear, pinning him immovably to the tree.

8

The Cunning Goblin

Peter, Sarah and Andrew were all awake very early on the morning following their imprisonment on Zarcos. All of them felt extremely stiff after the labours of the previous day and a night on hard wooden bunks.

'Ow, my arms don't half ache,' said Andrew.

'It's my back,' groaned Sarah as she tried to sit up. 'How are you, Peter?'

'Hm, not too bad, I think.' He staggered to his feet. 'Ouch! I spoke too soon. My knees hurt.'

'It's all that deck scrubbing,' said Andrew.

They spent the next few minutes stretching and stumbling around their cell trying to ease the aches and pains. But the thought of another day in the kitchens made them feel even worse.

'Look, we've just got to escape from this place somehow. I don't fancy being a slave for the rest of my life,' said Peter.

'Nor me,' declared Andrew. 'Anyone got any ideas?' He heaved at the bars on the window. 'No chance here; they're solid as a rock.'

'That would be too good to be true,' his brother commented. 'Anyway, it wouldn't help much. We've got to get Alena out as well, and we don't even know where she is.'

'The Grey Tower that creature said – wherever that is,'

said Sarah. 'I wonder if she's still got that jewel?'

'If that's what he's really after,' Andrew challenged.

'Well, I don't think it can be anything else,' Sarah retorted. 'I'm sure my dream was right.'

'You and your dreams.'

Sarah looked miffed and Peter intervened before she and Andrew could start squabbling. 'Come on you two. This isn't going to help. What we really need is to keep our eyes open today and see if we can find an escape route. Maybe we can find some way of talking to Alena as well.'

His brother and sister agreed and they said sorry to each other.

A guard came for them shortly afterwards and led them away to the kitchens where they were allowed to wash and have breakfast before being set to work.

* * *

That same dawn came as a mighty relief to Princess Alena. Never had she known a night as bad as the one that had just passed. Though she must have dozed at times, she felt as if she hadn't slept at all. She stared mournfully in the mirror at the dark shadows under her eyes.

'Ugh, what a sight!' she exclaimed. 'I don't want to go through that again.' She shuddered at the memory of the past hours.

However, morning light often fills the fearful with fresh courage, and she set her jaw firmly.

'Well, one thing is for sure: he's not going to get me that way,' she declared.

She ignored the dresses in the wardrobe and deliberately donned her old peasant's garb, then sat on the bed and waited to see what would happen. It wasn't long before the guard came and took her again to Gublak.

The goblin looked at her with half-amusement as she shambled into the room.

'Good morning. I trust you slept well,' he said.

'No I didn't and you know jolly well I didn't,' she snapped.

'I am sorry to hear that,' he lied. 'Maybe I can offer you breakfast to make amends?'

Princess Alena hesitated a moment, then glanced at the well-stocked table. She was hungry, and so with a curt nod and not another word she helped herself to the food. Gublak watched her in silence.

While she was on her last piece of toast, he started to talk again. He sat near the fireplace and spoke without looking at her.

'Last night I offered you vast wealth in exchange for the Star Stone, yet you refused to part with it. I must say I was surprised at your foolish reluctance – without which, by the way, one of my guards would not have died.'

The princess flashed him a sharp glance. 'I was sorry about that. But it was hardly my fault, was it? You shouldn't have tried to steal it. Why do you want the Star Stone, anyway? You're obviously rich. What's so special about this?'

He turned slowly to face her. His green eyes glittered and seemed to bore right into hers.

'You appear to know very little about the treasure you carry,' he said quietly. 'Deep mysteries and powers are hidden in the depths of its inner light. One such as I could unlock those secrets. That is why I wish to gaze upon it, to understand it, to . . . '

'You mean you wish to use it for your own ends,' she interrupted.

'Oh, yes, if you mean there is power in knowledge,' he breathed. 'But what is so wrong with that? After all, you had power when you were a princess.'

'Yes, but mine wasn't . . . isn't evil.'

The goblin shrugged. 'What is evil and what is good? I treat my servants well and I am generous with my favours. When I possess the Star Stone I shall be even more lavish towards those who serve me. Surely you are being evil by not letting me do that?'

The princess did not know how to reply. She was silent for a moment. Then she blurted out, 'I think what you're saying is a lot of nonsense. And you're still not having it.'

She walked over to the fire and stood warming her hands. Without turning she asked, 'Why don't you just kill me? Then you could have it, couldn't you?'

'Alas, you know that is not possible,' he replied with a sigh. 'The moment you were to die, the Star Stone would simply vaporise and be lost for ever.'

Alena had not known this and it gave her considerable comfort to know that whatever else happened, Gublak would not dare let her die. Such information might well prove useful.

The goblin decided to change his approach. 'Why do you cling on to this jewel? Why is it so important to you?' he asked. 'I am not sure you even know why you have it.'

'I've been taught never to give it away,' she said slowly, 'because if I do, I shall cease to be a princess and I shall lose my name.'

Gublak's eyes gleamed. 'What utter rubbish!' he cried scornfully. 'Superstitious nonsense. As if your name depended on that!'

Princess Alena turned on him hotly. 'Well, that's what I've been told. Why should I believe otherwise?'

'My dear child, has it never occurred to you that your name is what *you* call yourself? It does not exist just because of your birthstone. If that is all it does for you, you may as well sell it straight away.'

His words touched something in the princess. She felt confused. 'I . . . I . . . don't know about that.'

Gublak followed through quickly.

'Listen, I admire your independence – the way you ran away from home to choose your own life. That is the mark of a real princess. It has nothing to do with this . . . this Star Stone. You could prove the truth of my words simply by removing it now. In fact, that would show even more how much of a princess you really are.'

The goblin's persuasive tongue was having its effect. Princess Alena moved quietly to the window and stared out over the courtyard below for a long time.

* * *

The Urgils were not so strict with the children on this

their second day and they found that at times they could whisper together. Also, while they were carrying out their chores they were beginning to get some idea of the layout of their part of the fortress. The kitchens proved to be only one short flight of steps below the main courtyard. This was surrounded by a covered walkway off which were several entrances into other parts of the castle. Many windows and lofty towers overlooked the square.

All this the children observed when the Urgils marched them up the steps and across to a side gate. From there they were ordered to carry provisions into the castle from wagons that journeyed to and from *Grimwolf* throughout the day.

In an unguarded moment on his way up from the kitchens Andrew seized his opportunity to slip away and spy out the land. He ducked behind the low wall that supported the colonnades of the covered walkway. Keeping down, but peering about occasionally, he crept the length of the courtyard.

He had almost reached the far end when he spotted a movement at one of the first floor windows. To his delight he recognised Princess Alena. Would she see him? Throwing caution to the wind he stood and waved. For a moment there was no response. Then she spotted him. He saw her hand give a surreptitious little flutter in answer.

Just then he heard the angry shout of an Urgil who was scuttling across towards him. The guard dragged him by his ear back to work and Andrew received quite a few blows for his courage. But he'd found out something very important. They knew now that the princess was not kept permanently locked in the tower.

Princess Alena's heart leapt when she saw Andrew. His eager wave gave her new hope. She was sad when he was caught so quickly, but it filled her with fresh determination. She turned on Gublak.

'I want my friends released,' she demanded. 'You've no right to keep them like slaves.'

The goblin blinked but was not thrown off balance.

'But of course,' he replied smoothly. 'Though "friends" is rather a grand term for children you hardly know, isn't it? Commoners at that. Nevertheless, they will be released – the moment you hand over the Star Stone. Otherwise, they remain victims of your, um, self-ishness, don't they?'

She shrugged her shoulders. 'You're wasting your time. I'm not going to let you have it and that's that.' She glared at him with her hands on her hips. 'So what happens now? Are you going to lock me up again?'

'Why, no. As a princess you are perfectly free to roam the grounds. You shall not try to escape, of course, nor make any contact with those commoners. But I wish you to enjoy my hospitality. It is, after all, the least one member of royalty can do for another.'

Princess Alena shuddered at this comparison between Gublak and herself.

'I will see you at lunch,' he went on. 'And please,' he gave a disdainful glance at her frock, 'do try to dress as is becoming for a princess!'

Later, she sat alone on a wall in the garden and gazed at the Star Stone. The beautiful blue light twinkled in its depths and she felt strangely encouraged by its glow. But then other lights flashed in her head and her eyes began to sting. She wiped them, and the Star Stone seemed to grow very dull. She heaved a great sigh and replaced it in her dress.

After lunch, Gublak took her on a tour of his treasure stores. Somewhat in two minds, she had nevertheless dressed herself in one of the gowns that he had provided for her. She had chosen a stunning blue creation and Gublak had sounded appreciative.

He had not in the least exaggerated his wealth. The sheer quantities of treasure left her quite breathless. Gold seemed to drip from the walls and spill over the floors of the vaults. Gemstones glittered from all directions – fiery rubies, cool sapphires, sparkling diamonds and many others she hardly recognised.

'Of course, you are used to this sort of thing,' the goblin said with an airy wave of his hand.

'Oh, yes,' replied the princess without much conviction. The truth was that she was given very little access to the royal treasures back home. Something about 'when she was old enough'. In any case, she doubted whether the palace had anything like this kind of wealth.

Gublak encouraged her to play with the treasures. She tried on coronets, smothered her fingers with jewelled rings, hung dozens of solid gold necklaces around her neck. All the while he flattered her beauty and 'wise choices'. He told her she seemed to be in her natural element.

One thing particularly entranced her. She came across a set of puppets made of gold and silver with gems for eyes and operated by gold wires. The skilful workmanship made them seem almost lifelike.

'Oh, they're beautiful!' she exclaimed. 'Can I play with them for a while?'

'My dear princess, you can play with these and many, many other treasures.' He opened a door revealing a whole room full of such toys. She gasped and made to go in, but he checked her with his arm. 'However, I regret I must say again that the price for all this is one Star Stone.'

She turned away sadly and was sullen from then on and would not speak. Gublak smiled to himself.

That evening she was returned to the Grey Tower. All her memories of the previous night came flooding back as she lay trembling in bed, waiting for the terrors of the dark. But they did not come this time, and soon she was fast asleep.

Yet the evil magic had more than one way of working on her. She dreamed of possessing vast treasures, of having the freedom to do whatever she wanted. She imagined travelling the world in a golden coach. At one point she even thought of having Peter, Sarah and Andrew along as friends to share the toys. Then again, she was not sure if she knew them well enough or if they would be able to appreciate such things. No, she would have to choose her friends with care – people who would respect that she was a princess because she wanted to be. Maybe Peter and Andrew could be her servants, and Sarah her handmaid. . . .

Her dreams came to an end with a picture of a smiling Gublak ushering her into a vast room of sparkling treasure. In her hand was a golden puppet, while in his hand was a rather dull looking piece of glass on a silver chain.

9

Gublak Changes

The following morning, far away on the mainland and beyond the mountains, Oswain woke bleary-eyed, feeling that he had hardly slept at all. He glanced around the dimly lit room. To his alarm, Brankleshanks was nowhere to be seen and nor were his weapons. In an instant Oswain threw off his sleepiness, leapt to his feet and made for the door of the Dweorg's den.

Outside, the fresh morning sun filtered through the misty beeches of Moonwood, casting long shadows on the russet ground, but Oswain had no eyes for the beauties of the new day. Glancing this way and that, his face grim and anxious, he searched for signs of the Dweorg.

Then, in the misty morning light, he saw the Dweorg limping through the woods towards him.

'Where have you been?' Oswain demanded, his eyes narrow with suspicion. He saw that the crossbow was slung over the Dweorg's shoulder and the axe tucked into his belt.

'I may not be able to walk far, but walk I do. Do you begrudge me the fresh air?' the Dweorg answered.

'I thought Dweorgs preferred tunnels to woodland paths,' said Oswain.

'When the tunnels are closed the paths must needs do,' retorted the Dweorg.

Oswain made to reply but checked himself. He was,

as Brankleshanks correctly judged, anxious to be on his way.

So, after a hasty breakfast, Oswain began to walk westwards into the mountains with Brankleshanks riding piggyback in a sling harness on Oswain's shoulders. Although the Dweorg wasn't heavy, Oswain had no pleasure at the thought of carrying him through the mountains and it was only his concern for Alena and for Grumble that urged him on. Brankleshanks was also fully armed, and Oswain was not.

* * *

Peter, Sarah and Andrew woke up determined to form an escape plan.

'Right,' said Peter. 'First of all, what do we need?'

'Food,' Andrew replied promptly.

Sarah sighed. 'All you ever think about is your stomach.'

'He's right, though,' said Peter. 'So we'd better start collecting some today. I think we'll have to find water as we go because we've nothing to carry it in. What else do we need?'

'Some way of getting out of here without being noticed,' said Andrew.

'How about hiding in one of the wagons?' Sarah suggested.

'No, too obvious. Anyway, they're driven by those Urgils. We wouldn't get far,' Peter replied.

'Even if we get away from here, we've still got to get

off the island. How are we going to do that?' Andrew asked.

'I think we've got two choices,' his brother answered. 'Either we find a boat and row across to the mainland. Or we stow away on *Grimwolf*. Whatever, we must get down to the harbour without being seen.'

'Or getting caught by those wolves,' Sarah added with a shudder.

The others agreed wholeheartedly but before they could say more the guard came to escort them to the kitchens.

On their arrival they found things very busy. The Urgils were obviously preparing for a big feast and were hurrying backwards and forwards. This resulted in nobody being much concerned about the children. They were simply sent into a side room filled with sacks of potatoes and ordered to keep peeling until told to stop.

It was while pulling the second sack from the pile that Andrew made his discovery. Set into the floor was an iron ring. He bent down and gave it a tug. To his delight a small trapdoor swung open revealing a cellar. The children crowded round and peered into the gloom. The floor was only about two metres below and Peter hardly hesitated.

'Watch the door, Sarah. I'm going down.'

'All right, but mind how you go. Look out for rats.'

'How are you going to get out again, Pete?' Andrew asked.

He thought for a moment. 'Push one of those sacks of spuds down and I reckon I can reach if I stand on it.'

Andrew nodded and with that Peter swung himself over the side and dropped with a thud onto the floor beneath. He disappeared from his brother's sight but was back half a minute later looking glum.

'Not much luck,' he said. 'It's only a storage cellar. I can't find any other exit. You'd better shove the sack down, Andrew, so I can get out.'

'Pity there's not a secret tunnel like you read about in books,' said Andrew when Peter had clambered back out.

'Hm,' Peter looked about him slowly. 'But it's given me an idea. Look, grab some empty sacks and see what food you can find. Don't forget some for Alena as well. We'll start by hiding it down there. And now, listen. . . .'

He unfolded a daring plan to his brother and sister.

* * *

Far away in the depths of Moonwood Grumble winced. There must be a way to escape, but pain clouded his mind. Something told him to give up and let his life fade away. Once more, he slipped into the darkness.

All night long he had drifted in and out of conscious-ness. Unable to move because of the iron ring and the arrow that pierced his ear, he knew that somehow he must get free and warn Oswain. In moments of con-sciousness he recalled what had happened after he had left Oswain to seek out the next part of the path. Just when he thought he was on the right track a terrible pain had stabbed his head, a pain so bad that it felt like a red hot needle. He had been thrown through the air and that was the last thing he remembered.

He came round again when it was light and someone had come with water.

'I do not want you dead just yet,' said the voice. 'You are my guarantee that Oswain will return this way. He thinks that you are ahead of him on the trail. I shall keep him thinking so. Then when he has his sister, and I have my revenge, your plight will ensure that he brings me back.' The Dweorg grinned. 'Then we shall see what your life is worth. I will offer it in exchange for the Star Stone that Oswain's sister wears.'

The mouse took the water gratefully. 'How did you know we would come this way,' he croaked.

The Dweorg looked smug. 'A simple plan, though a bit of a gamble, but it paid off. My brother sent a hawk to intercept the message that the palace had sent to Oswain. The bearer was destroyed and another message sent telling Oswain to travel in this direction. All it needed was a simple trail laid by me that would lead you to Moonwood – and that's where I had you. If Oswain wants to see either you or his sister alive, he will do as I say.'

The Dweorg turned to step out of the hollow tree. 'When I next see you I shall be the owner of the Star Stone. You had best hope that you are alive to see it, too. But then I may shoot all three of you,' he added as an afterthought.

*   *   *

Much to her surprise, Princess Alena was allowed to

breakfast alone. In fact, it was not until mid-morning that Gublak entered the room and found her sitting by the window. She heaved a great sigh as he approached but didn't turn to look at him.

'How much are you going to offer me today? Or are you going to nag me into selling it?' she asked.

Gublak smiled as he replied, 'On the contrary. I have changed my mind. I no longer wish to buy it.'

The princess shot him a surprised glance, then said warily, 'What do you mean?' To her annoyance she couldn't avoid the feeling that she was in danger of losing a bargain.

The goblin ambled across to the fire and stood with his back towards it, facing her.

'You appear surprised,' he said. 'Yet should you be? Do you not call yourself a princess? Well, I shall allow you to be one. No longer shall I seek to bribe you into selling me the Star Stone. Instead, I wish to propose – a partnership. Perhaps even one day a marriage.'

She stared at him incredulously.

'A . . . a . . . partnership? Marriage? You have to be jesting. How on earth could I ever love an ugly creature such as you? Never in a thousand years!'

Gublak was unmoved by her scorn. He came closer and addressed her in slow, deliberate tones.

'They say beauty is in the eye of the beholder. You describe me as ugly, but could it perhaps be that your eyes deceive you? I will demonstrate.'

He stared straight at her while removing something from his pocket. Between bony finger and thumb he held a small glowing glass ball which he slowly circled between his face and hers. The princess felt her head begin to spin and everything became fuzzy. Then her eyes cleared. She gave a start. Before her stood a fine handsome man, suave, smiling and clothed in blue. Of Gublak there was no sign.

'Who . . . who are you?' she stammered. 'What's happened?'

'I am Gublak,' replied the stranger. The voice was unaltered.

'But you can't be!'

'Did I not say that it may have been your eyes that were deceived? Only now are you seeing truly. Before this, you were blinded to the truth by your own twisted thoughts. I am indeed Gublak, and this is how I can appear to you for ever.'

The princess sat back weakly in her chair. She didn't know what to say. She rubbed her eyes in disbelief but still the handsome man remained. He spoke again.

'Freedom and wealth are yours, Alena. But what are they without someone with whom to share them? You are surely not such a selfish person as to want it all for yourself?

'Yesterday, when you were young – so much younger than now – I offered you the ability to make others rich by entrusting me with the Star Stone. I no longer ask that. Now you are of age. Now, I beg you only to share its power with me, so that together we may bring happiness to our subjects.'

His eyes were appealing, his voice gently persuasive. Princess Alena felt very strange and suddenly quite grown up. A daring vision of a new life with Gublak flooded her imagination.

'With our shared wealth and the power of the Star

Stone we shall live happily and bring pleasure to so many people,' he continued. 'You as my princess and I as your prince.'

Alena tried to pull herself together and remember that this was a goblin speaking. But the magic was powerful.

'Yet you still want me to give you the Star Stone?' she queried.

He drew back in mock horror. 'Dear princess, I should not ever demand such a thing of you again. All I ask is to gaze upon it from time to time. Should you ever permit me to *borrow* it that would bring me great joy, but I would not force you so to do.'

He gazed earnestly into her eyes.

'Say you will stay. Share my wealth. Be my princess.'

She groped for a reply in the face of his charm.

'B . . . b . . . but I'm already a princess in my own country. Surely I should return to my home?'

He looked downcast.

'Why should you leave? After all, didn't you run away, to find adventure? Now you have found it. You chose your path and it has turned out for the good. Why go back?'

'I don't know why I ran away,' she replied slowly. 'I'm very confused about all that.' She looked at him and felt very weak. 'I . . . I must think about what you say.'

'Of course, my dear,' the handsome figure replied. 'I shall leave you now to consider my offer.'

He walked towards the door and Alena felt like begging him not to go.

'By the way,' he said from the doorway, 'tonight I

have a pleasant surprise for you. Dress well for the occasion.'

With that he was gone. Alena gave a wistful sigh and wondered what she should do.

*   *   *

The guards were so lax because of their extra work that Sarah actually managed to slip upstairs from the basement for a while during early afternoon. It was then that she spotted Princess Alena wandering across the courtyard lost in thought. With a couple of quick glances around she sneaked behind one of the columns and in a loud whisper called to the princess.

'Psst. Alena!'

The princess gave a start and glanced around.

'Over here,' Sarah whispered. 'To your left. Just act natural and sit on the wall.'

Princess Alena followed the voice and obeyed, looking straight ahead.

'Listen, it's me. Sarah. Are you all right, Alena?'

She nodded, then said, 'Yes, but you're taking an awful risk speaking to me. I daren't stay here long.'

'I know,' said Sarah urgently. 'But listen, we've got an escape plan and you'll have to get ready for it. We're going to do it tomorrow. Can you come here in the morning? And can you wear something for travelling in? I won't tell you any more now 'cos I'd better be getting back before I'm missed. Anyway, that horrible creature might get it out of you.'

The princess hesitated before replying.

'I . . . I . . . don't know whether I want to escape,' she said eventually.

Unable to see the confused look on her face Sarah imagined the princess was simply scared. 'Don't be afraid,' she said. 'We'll get away with it, you'll see. Just be here tomorrow. If you can't, we'll wait till the next day, but we'll rescue you somehow.'

And with that she darted back to the kitchens, leaving Princess Alena even more confused and unhappy.

* * *

'I need a rest.'

Strong and healthy though Oswain was, carrying Brankleshanks into the mountains was hard work. He released the straps of the harness and let his load clamber to the ground.

'You make a good packhorse,' said Brankleshanks.

Oswain grimaced. Under the Dweorg's guidance he had left the outskirts of Moonwood and taken a little used gravel track that at first rose steeply and then wound steadily upwards alongside a deep ravine at the bottom of which ran a fast-flowing stream. Now they had veered left onto an open plateau dotted with rocky outcrops and this brought them to a place where four ancient tracks met. Here, Oswain called a halt.

He was beginning to wonder about the wisdom of taking the Dweorg with him but knew, too, that he could never have found this path by himself.

'Which way next?' he asked as he took a drink from his flask.

'This is the Starkhill crossing,' Brankleshanks answered. 'We bear right.'

Oswain looked doubtfully at the path. They had seen no sign of Grumble and he wondered just where his companion might be. 'I think it's time you told me how you came to know that my sister had been kidnapped,' he said.

'And if I refuse?'

'Then I shall leave you to find your own way home,' Oswain replied.

The Dweorg pursed his thick lips. 'Then I shall tell you,' he agreed.

They sat on an outcrop of rock.

'My brother in the north knows of my plight and of my desire for revenge. He has kept an eye on Gublak for many years and he sends messages to me, though there is little I can do with the information. Several days ago, he told me that he had spoken with gypsies and had discovered that they were part of a plot to capture a princess who was to be delivered to Gublak. He also knew from his visits to Elmar that the princess carried a Star Stone.'

'Alena,' said Oswain.

Brankleshanks nodded. 'Your sister. You can imagine my fury when I found out. Not only did Gublak have all *my* treasure but he would now have a Star Stone as well.'

Oswain nodded.

'When I saw you and your companion enter Moonwood, I did not know who you were, but conversation travels in the woods and it took me only a little while to work out that you were Princess Alena's brother, Oswain, sent in search of her. It was a piece of good fortune,' Brankleshanks lied. 'I saw my chance, for I knew where she would be taken and I knew too that you would have the strength to take me there.'

'Which is how you get your revenge and I rescue my sister,' said Oswain.

'Exactly so.'

Oswain was uneasy. 'You are aware that she bears a Star Stone. How can I be sure that you will not attempt to steal it?'

The Dweorg gave Oswain a shrewd look. 'You cannot know,' he said.

'Then why should I not leave you here?'

'You may try but I have not told you the whereabouts of your sister, and nor shall I until we arrive there. Nor will I tell you where your mouse companion is. Oh, yes, he is still ahead of us. You will not see him, but I know this country and I know exactly where he is.' He glanced at Oswain. 'You see, I do not trust you, Oswain, any more than you can trust me.'

'Then we must travel without trust as best we may,' Oswain answered, his face grim. 'Come on. I am ready.'

* * *

Grumble was conscious again. It would not be easy, he decided, but he must do it. Gritting his teeth he pulled his head away from the arrow. The pain where it pierced his ear was terrible.

'I can't do it,' he gasped. Tears came to his eyes and he found himself trembling with the pain. Yet beneath Grumble's gruff exterior lay great courage and loyalty. 'I won't let Oswain down,' he determined. Breathing hard, he prepared himself.

'I often grumble,' he said aloud. 'Now I will complain about these shackles. I am angry and, by Elmesh, I shall be free!'

With that, he gritted his teeth and flung himself forward. Lights flashed before his eyes and he felt a terrible tearing sensation in his head, but in that moment he knew he was free. In spite of some bleeding from his torn ear, he quickly recovered and set to nibbling through the rope that bound him to the iron ring. Breathing hard, and feeling sick but satisfied, he struggled to his feet and scrambled from the hollow tree into the daylight.

After the dankness of the tree the fresh air and light were wonderful, but after one deep breath, Grumble knew he had no time to stand and stare. He had to get word back to Trotter as soon as possible and that meant finding Mumble. Praying that somehow Elmesh would guide him on the right path, and in spite of his injury, he scampered off just as fast as his legs could carry him.

* * *

The surprise that Gublak had promised took place that evening when Princess Alena was ushered into the great hall. She found it filled with Urgils dressed in their best uniforms. The children were there all spruced up, as was Captain Gaspar and, of course, Gublak himself.

To the princess he still appeared as a handsome prince, though to everyone else he was nothing but an ugly goblin. Princess Alena's heart fluttered as he approached.

'Alena, you look wonderful. Allow me, please, to explain all this.' He gestured around the room. 'I have laid on a party for you to make up for the one you missed on your birthday. I do hope you will enjoy it.'

He turned to the assembled company and gave a signal, at which the Urgils gave three cheers and raised their glasses in her honour. Princess Alena didn't know what to say and she flushed with embarrassment. Gublak took her arm and escorted her to a table overflowing with fine food. Musicians began to play and the feasting began.

Only Peter, Sarah and Andrew looked miserable.

'What's up with Alena?' whispered Andrew. 'Why's she looking so happy with that revolting creature?'

'I don't know,' replied Sarah. 'I just can't understand how she could let him touch her. I'd hate it. Ugh!'

'Look, she's joking with him now,' Andrew observed. 'And . . . and she's showing him the Star Stone.'

'Oh, please don't let her give it to him,' cried Sarah.

'She's been entranced,' said Peter grimly, as the memory of his previous experience with Hagbane the Shadow-witch flooded into his mind. 'Come on. We've got to interrupt this.'

The children made their way across to the couple.

'Hello, Alena,' said Peter. 'Happy late birthday. Though it can hardly be happy when we're all kept prisoners here, can it?'

The princess looked irritated at his interruption.

'I think it is very kind of Gublak to do this for me. And actually I'm quite enjoying myself,' she said primly. 'At least, I was until just now.'

Gublak smiled into her eyes. 'I do not think Peter understands, do you? That is the problem with these commoners.'

'I think I understand very well,' Peter exploded. 'You've got Alena under a spell, you evil creature.'

A flicker of emotion flashed across the goblin's face but he remained smiling.

'I do not wish to be rude in the presence of the princess, but it does seem you lack the party spirit, young man. I think you should depart.' He motioned to a guard nearby. 'These commoners are leaving us. Will you kindly escort them to their quarters?'

A pang of conscience struck Princess Alena and for a brief moment she knew the truth. In that instant she recalled Sarah's words and resolved to meet the others on the following day. But Gublak's spell was so powerful, and she had become so weak, that she could find nothing to say. The children looked back at her with despair as they were led away.

'I have a present for you,' said Gublak immediately they were out of sight.

He presented her with a large, gift wrapped parcel which, when she opened it with eager fingers, turned out to be the golden puppets she had so desired the day before. Her eyes sparkled with delight, and she thought no more of her friends.

That night Princess Alena dreamed again, and in her

dreams she heard the jabbering voices growing louder and louder. Then she saw accusing fingers wagging at her. The voices nagged on and on. She began to recognise them as those of her nanny, her teachers and her parents. Their faces appeared and were angry as they scolded her. It seemed to the princess as if that was all they had ever done. She pressed her hands to her ears and squeezed her eyes shut tight. All she wanted to do was be free of them and have her own life.

Beckoning in the dark was Gublak, tall and handsome, and she found herself running in slow motion towards him. She felt herself about to fall into his outstretched arms.

* * *

While she slept, Gublak had a visitor. It was Crow. He landed upon the table and let fall from his beak a rolled parchment scroll tied with red ribbon.

'This, Master, is all you require,' he cawed.

Gublak took the scroll and unfurled it.

'Excellent, excellent,' he muttered as his greedy green eyes scanned the contents. 'The Star Stone is within our grasp.'

10

The Scroll

As they were later to discover, darker powers than either the children or Princess Alena could imagine were at work behind Gublak's greed. It was of little interest to those powers whether or not the goblin came to possess the Star Stone, for they knew it would never serve the cause of evil. What they desired was that the princess should give it up, for then the royal line of the West would break and she herself would then serve their evil purposes.

This Trotter found out, many miles distant, as he sat by Elmere in the enchanted glade of the Great Forest of Alamore.

'The dark powers seek to destroy the noble and pure,' Trotter spoke gravely. 'In their wickedness they try to make the innocent evil like themselves. They seize any opportunity, find any chink in the armour. I suspect the princess, Alena, has long been watched for such a moment as this.'

Stiggle, the weasel who was chief officer of the guard, replied with quiet wisdom. 'Darkness is not the whole truth, my Lord. One day it will be revealed as only a passing lie. The pure love of Elmesh will rule for ever, serene as Elrilion itself.'

Both turned their furry snouts to the night sky, looked long at the star so named and felt its wondrous power.

'You are right, Stiggle,' Trotter smiled. 'There is indeed hope. But Elmesh gives his subjects the freedom to choose – good or evil. Princess Alena also must choose, and we must not try to protect her from that choice.

'Yet, I think she may receive some help even today,' Stiggle answered. 'For I feel in my fur that a lot will happen before the sun sets.'

* * *

Mumble was unsure what to do. He could see the first faint light of morning breaking on the horizon. Should he start back to the Great Forest? Fumble would be waking and for him it would be the fourth day with no news. What would he do? Would he wait for a message from Mumble? Would he race back to the forest? Mumble twitched his whiskers and smiled to himself. He could hardly imagine Fumble racing anywhere!

The sun rose in a blaze of golden fire and Mumble made up his mind. He would go back. Yet scarcely had he started when he heard a cough followed by a groan. Curious, he turned to investigate.

'Grumbleisatu?' he called.

He was answered by a croaking gasp and the next moment he saw none other than Grumble crawling towards him.

'Grumble, wasamarra? Wasappened?' he cried.

'Oswain in trouble. A Dweorg . . . Brankleshanks . . . shot me . . . taking Oswain to Alena . . . but wants the

Star Stone for himself . . . treacherous . . . may try to kill Oswain,' the mouse spluttered.

Mumble looked with horror at his bedraggled companion. Grumble's fur was matted and torn and dried blood covered one ear. He was clearly exhausted.

'Youmusrest,' he mumbled. 'Ilokaferyou.'

Grumble shook his head. 'No, you must go on . . . as fast as you can. Find Fumble . . . get back to Alamore . . . tell Trotter that Oswain's been sent off course . . . false message. He'll know what to do.'

'Butwhaboutyou?'

'What? Oh, I'll be all right. I just need to rest,' said Grumble. 'Now off you go – and try just for once to speak clearly, will you?'

Mumble looked doubtfully at Grumble and then smiled. If his companion was well enough to nag him, then he would make it through. Feeling better, he raced off on his mission, leaving Grumble to have a well-earned rest.

* * *

Princess Alena had been unsure what to wear on the morning following her party. On the one hand she now wished to please Gublak but she also wanted to be suitably clothed for a possible escape. In the end she chose a smart leather jerkin and trousers, boots, and a white blouse.

Gublak did not look quite as handsome when he walked in after she had breakfasted, but this barely registered with her. What caught her attention at once was the large, black bird he had with him. She leapt to her feet.

'Crow!' she cried. 'Where have you been? What are you doing here?'

'Good morning, Mistress,' he cawed in response and cocked his head towards Gublak.

Before the goblin could utter a word, realisation dawned on Alena.

'It was you!' she exclaimed furiously. 'You led me into the trap. You horrible traitor! And I trusted you. . . .'

For a moment she was beside herself with rage and the bird cowered behind Gublak, fearing that she might tear him wing from wing.

The goblin raised a hand. He spoke gently. 'My dear Alena, believe me it was necessary. If there had been another way less distressing to you, we would have used it.'

'Don't try to get round me like that,' she cried. 'I see it all clearly now. Crow is in your employ. He was your tool to get me here and persuade me to part with my Star Stone. Well, that's that. I shall never give in to you. Do you hear? Never! And I can see you for what you are, you ugly, fat, green goblin!'

Sharp pains stabbed her mind at that moment. She sat down clutching her head and burst into tears. Gublak and Crow waited until her sobbing subsided. The bird spoke: 'Mistress, what you say is true, but not all the truth. If I had not acted as I did, something awful would have remained hidden from you until, when you found out, it would have been too late.'

'What Crow says is correct,' continued Gublak. 'When

I offered to purchase the Star Stone from you it was because I already knew it was worthless to you. Yet I felt pity and love for you, and I desired to share my wealth and reign with you because . . .' he paused, 'because otherwise you would have nothing.'

'What do you mean? I don't know what you're talking about,' she snivelled. 'I have plenty of things at home.'

The goblin shook his head with pity, then lifted her chin and looked her straight in the eye. 'You have no idea, have you? The truth is, Alena, you were not born a princess at all.'

A stunned silence greeted his words. Princess Alena's mind whirled. This was the last thing she had expected to hear.

'You're lying,' she eventually whispered, though without much conviction.

'Unfortunately not,' Gublak replied solemnly. He drew from his robe the rolled parchment and laid it on the table before her. 'Read this for yourself.'

Hesitantly, she unrolled it and read:

In the seven-hundredth year from the foundation of Elmar, a girl-child of unknown name and parentage is hereby adopted by their royal persons, King Argil and Queen Talesanna of the Wester Lands, resident in the royal city of Elmar. The child will be known henceforth as Alena, that is Star-born.

It was signed by the clerk to the royal court and had the official seal. There was no doubt that it was genuine.

The information hit the princess like a thunderbolt.

She dropped the scroll and stared blankly at the table as her world fell apart. 'Of unknown name and parentage . . .' She was not really a princess at all. She was a nobody.

For all these years she had been made to live a lie. The airs and graces, the palace life, the clothes, they were all a sham. How she had tried to impress Gublak with her royal blood when all along he knew the truth. Why had nobody ever told her before? What a fool she felt!

Gublak was speaking again.

'You understand now that the Star Stone is but a useless charm. It cannot make you a princess when you are not. What value is a Star Stone to one who is not really Star-born?'

'What can I do?' groaned the princess in despair. 'I have no name of my own. No real parents. I've lost everything. Oh, why did you have to tell me this?'

'All is not lost,' replied Gublak. 'For have I not said you can choose to be a princess? I offer you the opportunity to do that. You may not have been born a princess, but you have shown the qualities of a ruler. By running away from home you have chosen your own pathway and fate has led you to me. I can give you wealth and power. You have earned this. You need no Star Stone. Let us put its powers to other uses, by all means, but let it not bind you to a false past any longer.'

'You can have it for all I care,' she said sadly. 'What's the point of keeping it?'

Her words were like music in Gublak's ears. His greedy eyes lit up and he rubbed his spiny fingers together in eager anticipation. His hands stretched towards her neck.

'Do you really mean that?' he breathed.

But the evil in Gublak had gone a little too far. Princess Alena glanced up just as his hands reached for the silver chain and, in that fraction of a second, she saw the depth of his greed. His eyes, hard and cruel, were filled only with intense craving. They frightened her and she drew back with a shudder.

'I . . . I . . . do, but not quite at this moment,' she stammered. 'I need a little time to think, to be alone. This has been a great shock to me.'

The goblin quickly hid his disappointment. 'But of course,' he shrugged. 'Though let it not be too long. I would like you to enjoy your privileges as my princess as soon as possible.'

'I'll take a walk now if you don't mind,' she replied, rising shakily to her feet. Gublak and Crow watched as she left the room.

'Do not worry, Master. There is no fight left in her. What will you do with her once the Star Stone is yours?'

'I have not decided,' the goblin replied. 'I may have her killed, or she may be useful to me in some way. We shall see. Either way, it will not be long now.'

Out in the courtyard an anxious Princess Alena looked about her. There was no sign of Sarah. Round and round she strolled, then, aware that Gublak and Crow might be watching from the windows, she made to pass through one of the gates leading into other parts of the fortress, but instead ducked behind the low wall, as Andrew had done. She crept along until she reached the corner, then got the shock of her life as Sarah's face appeared from the other side so suddenly that they almost bumped noses. She stifled a scream.

'Shush,' urged Sarah and squeezed her hand. 'Well done. Come on, this way.'

Princess Alena hesitated.

'What's wrong?' asked Sarah.

'I don't know,' she replied. 'I don't know what to do.'

She tried to explain as quickly as possible what had happened to her.

'Listen,' Sarah said when she had finished. 'This is all too much for me. All I know is that this goblin, Gublak or whatever he calls himself, is evil and if he gets his hands on your Star Stone something terrible will happen. You mustn't let him have it. You've got to come with us, Alena.'

'I suppose so,' the princess replied. 'But what's the point? I don't know who I am any longer. I feel I want to give up.'

'But that's just what he's trying to make you feel,' Sarah insisted. 'Now come on, before somebody catches us.'

With great reluctance Princess Alena followed Sarah around the wall and downstairs into the corridor leading to the kitchens. There they were met by Andrew.

'Quick, in here.' He shoved the princess without ceremony into the potato store room and pulled the trap-door open.

'Down you go. It's all right. It's quite safe.'

She hesitated a moment before obeying. Andrew followed and closed the door. They were only just in time, for a guard came past and demanded to know from Sarah where she had been.

'I can't see my brother Andrew anywhere,' she said truthfully.

The guard uttered a curse. 'That little troublemaker's run off again. Just wait till I get my claws on him.' He called to the other guard who was on kitchen duty. 'Hey, Gurk, that brat's on the run again. Come on, we'd better catch 'im before 'is Eminence finds out.' He turned to Peter and Sarah. 'And don't you try anything funny while we're gone.'

The children nodded innocently, but as soon as the Urgils had left they began to rush around the kitchen. Sarah spread old sacks everywhere and scattered firewood while Peter heaved a large barrel of cooking oil onto its side so that it ran all over the wooden floor. They ladled more oil onto the tables and splashed it over the walls.

'This had better work,' muttered Peter. 'You ready, Sarah?'

She nodded and ran to the door. Her brother took a stick from the woodpile. He thrust it into the fire until it was well alight, and then touched a piece of oil-soaked sacking with the flame. For one instant nothing happened. Then the oil caught. They watched for a few seconds as the flames spread, then darted next door into the potato room. Peter wrenched open the trapdoor and Sarah held it at an angle while he manoeuvred a sack of potatoes across the lid so that it would be hidden once it was closed. Then they both slipped down to join Andrew and the princess.

Above them, flames ran across the floor and licked up the walls. Within minutes the kitchen was a roaring inferno. Wooden beams crackled and sparks flew. Tongues of fire began to spread into the passageway and the door frame of the potato room caught light.

Down in their cellar smoke started to curl through the cracks between the floorboards and the children could hear a sullen roar as the fire grew in its intensity.

'Oh dear, what have we done?' wailed Sarah.

11

Escape

The first the guards knew of the fire was a cloud of thick black smoke billowing from the staircase that led to the courtyard. They immediately raised the alarm and other Urgils came running from all parts of the fortress. Gublak himself, accompanied by Crow, hurried to find out the cause of the commotion. As soon as he realised what was happening he barked a series of orders to his guards. His mind leapt to the obvious conclusion. The children had started the fire as a distraction in order to make their escape. He was consumed with a cold fury that this should happen just as the Star Stone was within his grasp.

'They won't get far,' he snarled. 'Ulris will see to that. Then they will pay dearly for their folly.'

He called out the wolf pack and rapidly explained what had happened. At once the wolves, led by Ulris, raced through the fortress gates and began to snuffle about for the scent.

Meanwhile, the guards were doing the best they could to contain the fire. There was very little water available in the fortress so they used axes to hack away all the wood surrounding the exits to the kitchens in the hope of preventing the fire from spreading. It was difficult work, for the heat was intense and the smoke suffocating.

An almighty crash signalled the collapse of the roof. A fiery fountain of sparks cascaded over the toiling Urgils and threatened to set fire to the adjoining rooms. They had to use what water was available to douse the floors. This may have saved the children's lives, for some of the water flooded across the floor of the potato store and prevented it from catching fire.

Grim-faced, Gublak watched the blaze from the courtyard above. He would show no mercy to those children when Ulris caught them. The leader came panting back to his master.

'There is no scent or trail, your Eminence,' he growled. 'I do not believe they have left the castle.'

'Then they are hiding somewhere,' Gublak answered. 'Search the grounds and every room.'

He himself went down the stairs to the corridor that led to the remains of the kitchens. The two guards who had been on kitchen duty were still fighting the blaze, though it was now burning less fiercely. Gublak demanded to know what had happened. In the darkness of their cellar the children listened with bated breath as the guards recounted the events leading up to the fire.

'They have tried to thwart my plans. Well, they shall not escape. I shall burn them alive when they are caught,' growled the goblin.

'Maybe they've all perished in the fire, Sir,' ventured Gurk.

The goblin spoke with an icy rasp. 'If they have then you shall undergo the same fate.' The Urgils shuddered. 'But I don't think so. The wolves and guards are searching every room. They will soon be found. As for you, I will decide your punishment when they are caught.'

The children and the princess heard the sound of the soldiers' rapidly retreating footsteps followed by the slow tread of Gublak.

'I reckon it's now or never,' whispered Peter as soon as all was quiet.

'What about the wolves?' asked Sarah.

'You heard what he said. They're searching the castle. This is probably the only chance we're going to get,' said Andrew. 'We'd better take it.'

'Right then, give me a moment to open the trapdoor,' said Peter.

He groped around until he found the sack of potatoes they had positioned underneath the trapdoor. Balancing himself on it precariously, he pushed up at the flap.

'It won't budge,' he gasped. 'It's stuck or something.'

'Here, let me help,' Andrew volunteered. He joined his brother on the sack but he was not tall enough to reach. Nor, for that matter, was Sarah.

'Oh dear, what are we going to do?' she cried.

'Alena, you're nearly as tall as Peter. You'd better give him a hand,' Andrew said.

The princess sat huddled in a corner, shivering. She did not answer.

'Alena, where are you?' Peter demanded.

'Over here,' she stuttered.

'What's the matter?'

'I'm scared.'

'Well, come on, pull yourself together and help me get this open.'

Sarah reached for the princess's hand in the dark and pulled her across to Peter. Somehow, between them they managed to get her onto the potato sack and Sarah and Andrew did their best to hold them both steady.

'Now push,' gasped Peter. 'Come on, push hard.'

The trapdoor began to open with their combined efforts and the four of them were immediately sprayed with a dirty mixture of ash and water.

'Ugh,' cried Andrew. 'I've just got a faceful.'

'Well, you'll have to put up with it for the moment,' said Peter. 'Now, I'll try to hold this open while you climb out, Alena. All right?'

He pressed up with all his might as she released her hold and tried to climb through the gap. She scrabbled for a grip while Peter gritted his teeth and bore the weight of the lid and, of course, the potato sack that still rested on top of it. His back and arms were in agony, and the sweat stood out on his forehead. He couldn't last much longer, but the princess did not have the strength to haul herself out.

'I can't do it,' she gasped in fright. 'I'm slipping.'

'Put your feet on my shoulders,' said Sarah. 'Go on. I'll hold you.'

It worked, and somehow she just managed to squeeze out. She was barely in time, for Peter's strength gave out and he collapsed on top of his brother and sister. Up above, Princess Alena heaved the sack off the trapdoor and soon had it open. Moments later, all four stood in the smoke-blackened room. They were absolutely filthy because of the water and ashes.

'Well done, Alena,' said Peter. 'We'd never have got out without you.'

She gave him a watery smile. 'You'd never have been here in the first place if it weren't for me,' she said.

'Never mind all that,' Andrew interrupted. 'We'd better get a move on. Everybody got their food sack? Come on, let's get out of here.'

The four crept stealthily along the corridor. They hardly dared breathe and expected to be seized at any moment. Up the short stairs they were able to spy out the land. The courtyard was empty and the side entrance through which they had lugged provisions was unguarded. Though only a few metres away, the open space between them and the gate seemed terribly exposed as they prepared to make a dash for it.

'You go first, Andrew, then Sarah. You after that, Alena, and I'll come last,' ordered Peter.

One by one, with a quick glance to the right and left, they darted across to the shelter of the archway.

'So far so good,' Peter panted. 'Now let's make for the coast as fast as we can. We'll have to go through the forest. No use going down the track. Let's just hope we don't meet any wolves.'

They began to descend the steep hillside and were soon deep in the undergrowth. Once under the cover of the trees they felt much safer and before long were scampering from tree to tree with ever-increasing confidence.

'That was a great plan, Pete,' yelled Andrew. 'Did you see the mess that fire made? Wonder the whole castle didn't burn down.'

'I wish it had,' he called back.

'Any idea how we're going to get off the island?'

'No, not yet. I just hope we can find a boat somewhere.'

'Do you think we've really got away with it?' puffed

Sarah. 'It seems too good to be true.'

'Yes,' cried Andrew. 'They'll still be searching all over the castle. It'll take them ages yet. And in the end they'll probably think we've been burnt alive.'

But he had reckoned without Ulris.

The cunning wolf was not leader of the pack for nothing. He was intelligent and quick-witted, as well as a ferocious fighter. Leaving the others to search the fortress, he padded back to the remains of the kitchen – and there he found what he was looking for. Footprints in the wet ashes. It took him only moments to work out how the children had foiled everyone. With a snarl he bounded up the stairs and leapt into the courtyard where he raised a bloodcurdling howl of alarm.

Wolves came leaping down corridors and through doors in answer to his call. Gublak leaned from a window.

'What is it, Ulris?' he demanded.

'They have fooled us, Eminence. They were hidden in the cellar and have fled while we looked elsewhere.'

'Then after them!' cried Gublak. 'But bring them back alive. I wish to supervise their deaths personally. Away now!'

The wolf pack tore through the gates at his command and were soon hot on the trail.

Far below, the children heard Ulris's alarm.

'They've found out,' Sarah cried. 'Now what'll we do?'

'Keep moving, faster,' said Peter grimly.

Princess Alena looked a picture of despair. Fear paralysed her legs and she sank to the ground.

'I can't go on,' she gasped.

'Don't be stupid,' Sarah screamed. 'Come on.'

She grabbed the princess's hand and yanked her to her feet so hard that she had no choice but to stumble on down the hillside.

'Faster,' urged Andrew. 'I can hear them.'

The howls of the wolves seemed to fill the air and terror lent wings to the children's feet. They fairly flew down the hillside.

All at once, they broke from the trees into a broad clearing, and the ground fell away sharply before them into a steep ravine. By now, they were running so fast that it was impossible to stop and one by one they slithered and rolled to the bottom of the gorge. Fortunately, it wasn't too deep and, unharmed, they scrambled to their feet and ran blindly on, heedless of their direction.

It took only a few moments more for them to discover they were trapped. Straight ahead was a blank, grey cliff wall. They came to a standstill and looked wildly about them. On all sides the gully rose steeply. There was no way out.

'Now what do we do?' cried Princess Alena in dismay.

Before anyone could answer there was a crashing in the trees above them and the fearsome grey form of Ulris appeared on the lip of the cliff. His yellow eyes glinted as he sighted the children and his jaws slavered with anticipation.

'Ulris is not so easily fooled,' he grated. He motioned with his head and the pack spread out. They began to wind their way down the ravine towards where the children stood cowering in defeat.

12

The Whirlpool

'I told you to leave me behind,' Princess Alena sobbed. 'I didn't want to come with you in the first place. Now look what's happened.'

'Oh, don't be ridiculous,' Sarah scolded. 'We're all in this together, whether you like it or not.'

Huddled together, they watched as the hungry-looking wolves drew ever closer.

'Oh, please, Elmesh, Oswain, someone help us,' Sarah groaned.

'You sure we can't make a run for it, Pete?' Andrew muttered.

His brother shook his head. 'There's nowhere to go, is there?' He glanced back at the cliff in desperation – and then looked again in amazement. There, faintly etched on the rocky face, was the outline of a dove.

'Look, everybody,' he cried.

The others turned.

'Of course,' exclaimed Sarah. 'Come on. I know what to do.'

She ran to the cliff wall, reaching into her jerkin as she did so. Peter, Andrew and Alena watched in wonder as she drew out a long feather and with it swiftly traced the outline of a door on the rock. A moment later, the image of the dove vanished but a faint blue line remained shimmering on the cliff where Sarah had drawn.

'It's a door of some kind,' exclaimed Peter and he ran towards it.

He could see no way of opening it.

'Perhaps you have to say "Open, sesame",' Andrew suggested. He shouted, 'Abracadabra, open sesame,' at the top of his voice. Nothing happened.

'Don't be silly,' Sarah replied. 'It must be Elmesh's doing. This is *real* magic. Oh, if only we had Gilmere again.'

'But we have,' cried Peter with a flash of inspiration. 'Or near enough. What about your Star Stone, Alena? That could do it.'

'Oh that,' she sniffed. 'All that's done is cause trouble. It won't do any good.'

'Get it out, anyway,' Sarah urged.

'Well, all right. But we may as well give up, you know.'

She reached into her blouse and drew out the jewel. By now, the wolves were little more than a hundred metres away and were advancing on their prey at a steady lope.

Peter was urgent. 'Point it at the outline,' he said.

Princess Alena reluctantly did so, but nothing happened. Sarah was beside herself with exasperation.

'Oh, for goodness sake, Alena, believe in it, just for a moment. Come on, all of us.'

They concentrated hard and whether it was the threat of the wolves or something more, the princess did manage to believe in the Star Stone's power.

'Open in the name of Elmesh,' ordered Peter.

At once, a fiery blue beam blazed from the jewel and struck the faint outline of the door. It sparkled to life with an electric blue flame and before their wondering gaze a stone door swung open. There before them lay a tunnel, lit at the far end by a pale ghostly glow.

'Quick,' cried Peter. 'It's worked. Run for it!'

Ulris, who was at the head of the wolves and only fifty metres away, saw what had happened. With a snarl of fury he leapt forwards.

The children sprinted along the tunnel as swiftly as their legs could carry them, but the wolves were gaining. Faster and faster they ran. The howling and panting of their pursuers echoed off the passage walls and they seemed almost at the children's heels. Hopes that the magic door would keep the wolves out were dashed.

The pale light ahead grew closer and Peter wondered if it was simply daylight at the other end – in which case all would be lost. But it proved to be more daunting still, for the tunnel came to an abrupt dead end.

To their amazement, they saw that the light came from a rapidly whirling pool of water fed by a small waterfall gushing from the roof. There was no way forwards and the wolves were almost upon them.

'We must have to jump in the pool,' gasped Andrew.

'It's no good,' screamed Princess Alena. 'We're trapped.'

'Get in,' snapped Peter. 'It's got to be right. Come on, it's our only hope. Hold your breath.'

He gave the princess a shove and she fell with a cry into the glowing whirlpool, to be instantly swallowed up. Sarah and Andrew looked at each other for courage then plunged in together. Peter turned to find himself face to face with Ulris.

'There is no escape for you though, is there?' Ulris

snarled. He bared his fangs and advanced while the other wolves fanned out leaving the boy nowhere to go. There was only one thing for it: in sheer desperation Peter threw himself into a back-flip and plunged into the whirlpool, thinking for a brief instant that it was a good job he had been practising that dive all summer.

The water sucked him down at a dizzying speed. He tried opening his eyes for a moment but was dazzled by a kaleidoscope of rushing colours. His head span in the confusion of light and after that he simply lost consciousness.

Meanwhile, up above, a defeated Ulris growled with rage and watched as the light went out in the pool. Neither he nor any in his cruel pack dared venture into the swirling black waters that remained.

* * *

Peter stirred slightly and smiled to himself. He gave a contented grunt and snuggled into a more comfortable position on the soft surface. He felt warm and relaxed and half-dreamed he was adrift on a sunlit sea.

It was Andrew's shout that made him open his eyes. He gave a small start of surprise, for he found himself lying on sand. He jerked upright and looked about him to find he was on a gently shelving beach and small waves were lapping at the shore. The sound of splashing water behind made him turn to see a stream pouring from the rocky cliff and soaking away into the sand. Not far away lay his sister and Princess Alena. Andrew was already sitting up.

'Hey, Pete, what's happened to us? Where are we?'

'Haven't a clue,' he replied. 'Last thing I remember was being sucked down that whirlpool.'

'Me too.'

Andrew staggered to his feet and stumbled across to his brother. 'Are the girls all right?' He gave his sister a shake. 'Sarah?'

'Mm.' She smiled and stretched. 'I feel so nice. Are we in heaven or something?'

'No, I don't think so,' Peter replied. 'On a beach somewhere. I think we somehow got washed down to the shore,' he explained, and showed them both the stream.

'Well, thank goodness for feathers!' said Sarah.

'You never told us about that,' said Peter. 'Where did you get it?'

Before Sarah could explain, Princess Alena sat bolt upright. 'W . . . where are we? Where are the wolves?' she asked with alarm.

The others laughed. 'It's all right, Alena,' said Peter as gently as he could. 'We're safe now – at least, for the moment.'

They studied their surroundings. The food sacks had been washed down with them and by some miracle the food was dry. In fact, even their clothes showed no signs of having been drenched. As far as anyone could see they were still on the island, for the mainland was recognisable across the straits. None of them had any idea how long they had slept, but their stomachs told them lunch was overdue. So, before exploring farther they drank from the stream and ate some food.

'You know, this is all very nice,' said Peter, 'but we

really must get off this island. Somehow I don't think Gublak will have given up the search.'

'I agree,' Andrew said. 'For all we know they might be combing the island right now. They may even know about this stream.'

'Then what are we waiting for?' Sarah exclaimed in alarm. 'We must find a boat. It's too far to swim.'

They jogged down to the seashore in order to obtain a better view, but whichever part of the island they were on, it was completely deserted. The sand stretched monotonously in both directions until it curved away out of sight. Behind them, above the low cliffs, the forest rose dark and forbidding towards the summit. Somewhere just out of sight must be Gublak's fortress. The sky was clear blue and empty. There seemed no hope of escape.

It was just then that Andrew spotted something. 'Hey, look. Out there.' He pointed across the sea.

For a moment nobody could see what he was pointing at. Then they spied the graceful grey creatures leaping through the waves.

'Why, they're dolphins!' exclaimed Sarah. 'Look, there are four of them.'

'No, five,' Peter corrected. 'See?'

'They're coming this way,' yelled Andrew with excitement, and to their wonder the beautiful creatures drew right into the shallows. One of them, by far the largest, rose out of the water on his tail, as dolphins do, and waved his flippers. The children laughed. Then he spoke. The voice was unlike anything they had ever heard. They might have expected to hear a high-pitched squeak but instead it was deep and strangely musical, and reminded Sarah afterwards of a cello.

'We have heard your song,' he said, or rather hummed.

'What song?' Peter called, puzzled.

'Why, the music of the singing stone. Sweet it was, as the sound of the shimmering sea beneath a thousand stars. Haunting were its melodies, as moonbeams caressing a coral strand on a soft summer's night. How could we resist such rapturous harmony? We come to serve its call.'

'What's he talking about?' whispered Andrew to Peter.

'I'm not sure, but maybe he means Alena's jewel,' he replied.

As if in answer to the question, the dolphin spoke again. 'Which favoured one bears the stone? And what service may we bring?'

'Go on, Alena,' Andrew urged. 'It must be you.'

The princess stepped forward and spoke with some hesitation. 'I am Alena and I bear such a stone,' she said. 'We need to cross the sea to the mainland but we have, as you see, no means. If you could help us in some way we would be most grateful.'

The dolphin flipped beneath the waves and re-emerged with his companions only to repeat the action in a series of splendid dives.

'Our delight is boundless,' he sang at last. 'We shall bear you ourselves to the shore you seek. Come, sit upon our backs. And I, fair stone-bearer, would have you ride with me, if such privilege I may enjoy.'

The children waded out into the shallows and soon found themselves astride the backs of these magnificent creatures. The journey was enthralling. The dolphins carved effortlessly through the waves, at times leaping in graceful arcs and weaving between one another in criss-crossing paths like playful speedboats. The children, soaked to the skin and covered in sea spray, would not have missed the experience for anything. They laughed and screamed with delight at the breathtaking antics of their mounts.

Throughout the journey each of the dolphins hummed a continuous note which not only seemed just right for the child he carried but was also in perfect harmony with that of his companions. The music made the children feel very safe.

The approaching shore proved to be a rugged coastline rising at once to high mountains. There was no sign of habitation and before long they came to the shallow waters of a small pebbly bay where they came to rest. The four children, still wondering at their miraculous escape, slipped from the dolphins and thanked them. The leader of the school looked at them with friendly eyes.

'Farewell, good speed, my friends. May Elmesh guide your steps upon this foreign land. Let his music keep your hearts from fear. Maybe some day we shall meet again.'

With that the dolphins were off. The children waded to shore and waved wistful goodbyes as their friends cavorted northwards.

'You know, that really is some jewel,' said Peter to Alena. She gave him a weak smile and nodded thoughtfully.

The sun was still high, so the first thing they did was

let their clothes dry in its heat. Most of their food was ruined except for some fruit and cheese, but nobody was too worried. To be free from the island and Gublak was sufficient. They lay back, content to do nothing except chat about the dolphins and what it felt like riding them.

Suddenly Alena sat up, her face turning pale.

'What's up, Alena?' Peter asked.

She pointed to the sky at a black speck in the distance.

'I have a feeling that's Crow,' she said.

They watched as the bird grew smaller. It was heading back to the island.

'Then this isn't a place for us to hang about,' said Peter. 'Let's be on our way. Now!'

13

The Slabs of Dringol

A deep dark desire, as deep and as dark as the seeing well into which he gazed, burned in the heart of Dringol. What he saw filled him with unexpected pleasure as the vision of a Star Stone came within his reach.

Would his brother Brankleshanks mind? Would he ever know? Only if he, too, were to discover the children's escape with the princess. Only if he followed them and came upon Dringol. That must not happen, Dringol decided.

Yet Brankleshanks was his brother and was surely entitled to something for his pains, if only his revenge and maybe his treasure. Dringol returned his eye to the well. There he saw a ship and he knew it would sail south around Illian Head to the nearest deep water landing. He would signal Brankleshanks, *'Gublak is coming ashore and he has the princess with him.'* Only he doesn't. The princess is coming to Dringol and with her the Star Stone! The Dweorg's lips curled into a greedy leer as he plotted how to tell his half-truth.

Thus, in the late afternoon, Oswain and Brankleshanks were to receive a flashed message that made the Dweorg insist that they stop and turn their steps urgently south-east, for that was where they would find both the princess and the goblin. Wearily, Oswain protested that this was becoming a wild goose chase and they would be retracing half of their journey.

'I am sorry,' said Brankleshanks. 'Yet our quarry will be nearer than if we had continued this way – and we have time. They cannot land before tomorrow.'

'What about Grumble?'

The Dweorg shrugged his shoulders. 'Who is the more important to you?' he asked.

'That isn't a question I can easily answer,' Oswain acknowledged. 'But I guess Grumble would say I must stick to the quest to find Alena. He is probably right, but I don't like it.'

'I have lost sight of him,' Brankleshanks lied. 'He could be anywhere. But now we know where your sister is.'

Reluctantly, Oswain agreed and they turned towards the south-east, but he couldn't help feeling that he was betraying a friend.

* * *

Peter looked around him and sized up the land. The beach marked the bottom of a steep valley where a stream had slashed its wild way down the mountain-side. All around towering cliffs dropped sheer into the sea. The only way inland was to climb, following the rugged course of the brook.

'At least we won't be short of water,' Andrew said cheerfully as they scrunched up the beach towards the grassy lower slopes of the valley.

Peter didn't reply. He looked serious. A little bit of mountain walking had taught him how dangerous it is to lead an unequipped party even in familiar territory, let alone across unknown terrain, without map or compass. He was not even sure if this was the right way; it was just the only way. He tried not to let his feelings show.

'Come on, everyone,' he shouted. 'Let's keep together and get a move on. It's mid-afternoon already and we've a long way to go.'

A chorus of groans answered him but they did as he said.

At first, the journey was quite easy and they were able to tramp up the valley at a steady pace to the cheerful chatter of the stream as it wound between the boulders. However, their path soon began to rise and it wasn't long before everyone was puffing and blowing. The grass gave way to shattered rock and often they were having to use their hands to clamber over the larger boulders. In spite of this, they managed to keep going for about an hour before Peter called a proper halt.

'Phew, I feel done in,' exclaimed Sarah. 'I thought you were never going to stop.'

'Well, I wanted us to get a good start,' he explained. 'We'll not be able to go so fast from now on. You all right, Andrew?'

His brother's bright red face smiled back cheerfully. He was fine.

'How about you, Alena?'

She smiled a brief acknowledgement but did not look at all happy. The others gave one another knowing glances.

'Well, let's have five minutes' break, anyway,' Peter said.

The view was stunning. The valley fell away in a broad sweep of jumbled brown and grey rocks. Sunlight glittered on the water as it cascaded over ledges and boulders. Far below through the haze they could see the little pebble beach looking now no bigger than a cornflake.

'Any idea how far we've climbed, Pete?' asked Andrew.

'Difficult to say but maybe two hundred and fifty metres,' he replied.

He shaded his eyes against the sun and stared into the distance. The sea was misty blue and the horizon lost in haze but he could still make out the island and what looked like Gublak's fortress on top. He squinted to see more detail. A movement caught his eye. From around the northern tip of the island a dark shape was emerging. He kept silent and watched. Then it dawned on him. *Grimwolf* had set sail and was heading in their direction!

'On your feet, everybody,' he said quickly. 'They're after us.'

The others followed his gaze and needed no further encouragement to be on their way.

'I bet that's Crow's doing,' said Andrew with disgust.

In spite of feeling a bit stiff after their rest, the desire to increase the distance between themselves and their pursuers urged them on. But the mountain was slowing them down. It was growing very steep and they were having to clamber on all fours most of the time. Peter hoped they would not reach a point where ropes would be necessary. Their only hope lay in sticking by the brook. He glanced across at Alena. She looked very glum. Something was up.

It was as they reached a difficult part that the crisis broke. Peter had just helped Sarah and Andrew over a slippery slab of rock and was waiting as the princess attempted it. Her foot slipped and she stumbled.

'It's no good,' she cried in exasperation. 'I can't go on. I want to go back.'

The children were dumbfounded.

'You what?' said Andrew when he found his voice. He couldn't believe his ears.

'I want to go back. Do you hear?' she shouted at them.

'But they'll kill you,' said Andrew.

'Not while I have the Star Stone.'

'But he'll get it off you,' cried Sarah.

'Don't be a fool. He wants me to share it with him,' she responded. Her voice sounded strange as though she were not quite herself.

'But don't you realise it's all a trick?' said Peter.

'I shall be a great princess,' she exclaimed. Her face grew haughty. 'I shall have all I desire if I return.'

'But you're already a princess,' he insisted.

Alena sat down and tears came to her eyes. 'But that's the whole point. I'm not. Don't you see, I have nothing to return to? I'm an orphan. If I go with you I shall only be pretending to be a princess. If I return to Gublak at least it will be my choice.'

'But surely being adopted into the royal family makes you a real princess?' Peter persisted.

By now Princess Alena was growing hysterical. 'Oh, stop going on,' she screamed. 'You don't understand. I hate being adopted. I hate this mountain. I hate everybody! Now get out of my way. I'm going down.'

She rose trembling to her feet and made to depart, but Peter restrained her. He knew that one of the most important things on mountains was not to lose your nerve. He had to take charge. For a long tense moment the princess and he stared at each other. It was a battle of wills. Then suddenly she relaxed and collapsed into a tearful heap.

'Oh, I'm sorry,' she sobbed. 'But . . . it's these voices in my head. They keep saying things to me. I've heard them all the way up, ever since we left the beach, and I can't stand any more.'

'I knew something was wrong,' said Sarah.

'Why didn't you say so earlier?' Peter asked the princess.

'I don't know,' she wailed. 'I don't know anything any more. Why don't you go on and leave me behind? You'll be all right. It's me they want.'

'Look, let's not start that again,' Peter said in a matter-of-fact voice. 'Nobody is going back. We're here to rescue you and that's what we're going to do. So come on.'

Reluctantly she got to her feet.

'Right, now try that rock again.'

To her surprise the princess managed quite easily this time. She was beginning to respect Peter. To cheer her up, Sarah and Andrew sang their version of 'Ten green bottles' which was 'Ten green goblins standing on a ball'. She laughed and felt better.

Soon, however, their route became too steep for singing. In spite of this, Peter allowed only brief rests. It was no longer possible to see the beach and he wondered if the pirates had landed.

The sun was sinking fast and the air grew cool. Mist

shrouded the horizon far out to sea and shadows were beginning to fall. There was no wind and a heavy stillness hung in the air. The only sound was the chilly tinkle of the brook. Peter knew they could not go much farther before needing to find some shelter for the night. Thankfully, the head of the valley was just above them and it could be downhill after that.

However, when they reached the crest five minutes later it was just as though they had entered another world. Right before them, lying still and dark in the shadows thrown by the setting sun, was a calm mountain lake. This was the source of the stream they had been following. Rising from it on all sides but their own were steep slabs of fissured rock that appeared quite impassable.

Most daunting of all was the breathtaking sweep of a snow-covered hanging valley that stretched away to the distant skyline. It had been completely out of sight from below.

Peter's heart sank. There was no way they could hope to climb further that day. In fact, he couldn't see how they would ever cross the awesome slabs that lay ahead. It looked as though they were stuck – and the pirates could well be upon them by nightfall. Turning glumly to his companions he gave a shrug of despair. He felt like crying.

Just then, they heard a shout. Each one whirled round to see where it came from. Hearts thumped wildly. Surely the pirates weren't here already?

'Ho!' cried the voice again.

Striding with such ease across the slabs that you would be forgiven for thinking they were flat ground came a short, thickset human-like figure. He wore a sheepskin jerkin and leather breeches and was armed with a staff and a fearsome axe. A long sheathed knife hung from his broad belt and a crossbow was slung across his back.

'Why, it's a dwarf,' whispered Sarah, though he looked far too stern to be like anyone from a fairy story.

He drew near and stood, legs astride, before them.

'So, what are you strangers about, trespassing in my domain?' he demanded. His voice was deep and gruff. He didn't look at all friendly.

'Please, sir, we didn't know we were on anybody's private property,' Peter replied politely. 'We landed on the beach below and are travelling across the mountain to the land beyond.'

The Dweorg, for that of course was what he was, eyed him with suspicion. 'Why should you wish to come this way?' he questioned sharply.

'It seemed to be the only way,' the boy replied. He didn't feel it wise to reveal too much to this stranger. 'Actually, we're a bit lost. So, if you'll kindly show us the way we'll leave your land as soon as possible.'

'You are by the Slabs of Dringol,' the Dweorg replied. 'I am Dringol and this is my domain. None pass except with my permission, and that I give to few. Why should I grant you passage?'

Peter was at a loss for words. Sarah stepped forwards. 'Please, sir, we don't wish to intrude but nor do we want to go all the way back to the beach. Have pity on us and let us through.'

The Dweorg looked with interest at Sarah's blonde hair and then at the golden head of Princess Alena. His thick lips parted in a sort of smile.

'Very well. I shall grant your request. But it shall not be for nothing. What will you pay me for my pains?' His eyes gleamed. 'Gold I like, and silver, and jewels. Do you have any?'

The children shook their heads. Then Princess Alena thought of her Star Stone and was about to say something when Andrew gave her a sharp but sly kick in the ankle that made her cry out in pain.

'Sorry, I must have kicked something,' Andrew said. He bent down to where she was rubbing her ankle and whispered through the side of his mouth, 'Keep quiet about it. Say nothing.'

The Dweorg eyed them inquisitively.

'Are you sure you have no jewels for me?'

'The only thing we can offer is what food we have in our sacks,' said Peter with dignity.

The Dweorg looked disappointed and hesitated a few moments. Peter did not trust his cunning eyes. 'Very well. I shall take all you have as the price of a path.'

One by one they handed over their sacks. He flung them across his shoulders and then stomped off, leaving the children to follow. After skirting the lake for a while, he suddenly came to a halt. The children wondered what he was about to do. He turned to them.

'You cannot traverse the Slabs of Dringol but there is a path beneath the mountain that leads to the ridge. I shall take you that way.'

With that he tapped his staff against a rock. Immediately it rolled back to reveal a dimly lit tunnel. He strode in. The children hesitated.

'I do not wait for strangers,' he said. 'Come now.'

With much misgiving they entered the mouth of the tunnel. At once, the rock rumbled back into place, shutting out the daylight with a resounding crash. It felt as if the mountain had swallowed them. The Dweorg gave a hollow laugh that echoed and boomed along the subterranean corridors.

14
Riddles

The tunnel was lit by a flaming torch that Dringol removed from a bracket on the wall. It made spooky shadows dance on the rough-hewn rock. The four children waited in trepidation as the Dweorg's laughter echoed in the silence.

'Why are you afraid?' he boomed. 'I mean you no harm. Have we not struck a bargain? I shall honour the value of what you have paid me. Come, follow me.'

The children, with no choice but to trust him, began to file after the Dweorg. The tunnel was not very high and Peter had to stoop most of the way, which made it a very uncomfortable journey for him. Their path twisted and turned but all the while rose steadily. Every so often they would pass a blank black hole that indicated other tunnels leading off to the right or left. Where or to what they led, none could guess. They trembled with the knowledge that they were completely at the Dweorg's mercy.

Soon they were perspiring freely, for it was very warm under the mountain and Dringol was moving fast.

At length the path dipped slightly and they entered a lofty cavern from which several tunnels led off in different directions. Here the Dweorg stopped. He turned to the children and gave them a shrewd look from beneath his beetled brows.

'Many are the ways beneath the mountain and Dringol knows them all. But what if I should leave you now? Would you not be lost for ever – doomed to wander the nameless deeps of the earth till the end of time?'

The children said nothing. Then Peter spoke. He fixed the Dweorg with a solemn look. 'You gave us your word you would lead us to the top of the ridge.'

'Ah, my word. Yes, my word. As truly as you gave me yours, indeed. All you had to give was your food, eh?'

Peter felt uncomfortable under his piercing gaze. The Dweorg continued, 'Let us play a little game before we proceed. Do you like games? I will ask a riddle or two. And if you guess the answer correctly I will lead you further, but if not. . . .'

'But that's not fair,' interrupted Sarah.

'Hang on a moment,' said Andrew. He laid a restraining hand on his sister's arm. 'I think that's a smashing idea, Mr Dringol. Only let's make it more interesting. We'll ask a riddle as well, and, as you are older and wiser, we only have to answer yours if you can answer ours. And if you can't answer ours you must lead us on.'

The Dweorg looked irritated and Andrew wondered if he would take up the challenge.

'Oh, very well,' he snapped. 'But I ask mine first.'

Andrew agreed. The Dweorg peered at each of them in turn before speaking.

'From whom fly four
To Dringol's lair;
Green, fat and rich
Midst sea so fair?'

The children gave one another uneasy glances. They knew the answer and began to guess the Dweorg's cunning purpose. Dringol smirked. Andrew, however, was not to be outdone.

'Well, here's mine,' he said. 'What's the difference between a wet day and a lion with toothache?'

Dringol frowned and muttered to himself. The children waited anxiously as he strode round and round in small rapid circles. At length he stopped.

'I give up,' he said angrily.

'Then we don't have to guess the answer to yours,' said Peter. 'Now you must keep your bargain and lead us to the ridge.'

Dringol growled to himself but reluctantly agreed. They set off through one of the tunnels, the children almost running to keep up with him.

'Well done, Andrew,' Sarah puffed. 'Where did you get that one?'

'Christmas cracker,' he replied with a grin. 'Do you know the answer?'

'I think so,' she answered. 'Um, one is pouring with rain and the other is roaring with pain.'

He nodded.

On and on they hurried until the children lost all track of how long they had been under the mountain. There was nothing else to do but keep up with the flickering torch as it wound its way ever upwards along this endless corridor.

Seemingly ages later, they came to another cave in which a small fire burned. Dringol called a halt and promptly sat down. The others gratefully did the same. He opened the four sacks and spilled out the remains of the food on the ground.

'Hm, not a generous gift for such a journey,' he said as he eyed the few apples, pears and bits of cheese. 'But it will do . . . for the moment.'

The children and the princess were obliged to sit and watch as the Dweorg greedily devoured all the food. Not once did he offer them a bite. It made them realise how hungry they were and Peter wondered how they would survive the journey down the mountain without food.

Dringol licked his lips and eyed the children. 'Time for the next game of riddles, I think.'

Peter, Sarah and Princess Alena glanced at Andrew and hoped he had a good one ready. The Dweorg recited:

> 'Sails on the sea
> With jaws stained red,
> Who can this be
> The travellers dread?'

Sarah looked at Peter with dismay. The Dweorg knew too much. If they had to answer this one he would surely demand to know why they were running away. Then the game would be up. He would soon be after the Star Stone.

Andrew spoke up:

> 'A hiss, a bellow, and a "gloop",
> Four lines on yellow, then they stop.
> What is it?'

The Dweorg sank his head onto his chest as people do when they are thinking. He muttered Andrew's riddle over and over again to himself. Even Peter, Sarah and the princess looked puzzled. Andrew just smiled.

At last, the Dweorg leapt to his feet and glowered at him. 'I don't know,' he growled.

'Then lead us on, please, as we agreed,' Peter said quietly, though he felt afraid.

'Very well,' he snapped. 'But be warned: you shall not get the better of me again.'

With that he stomped off, leaving them to follow.

'Whew, well done, Andrew,' whispered Peter. 'But what was the answer? I couldn't work it out.'

Andrew chuckled. 'Oh, it's easy. It's an elephant skating on a bowl of cold custard!'

Some while after, they began to climb a long wide staircase. Up and up it went as far as the flickering torch would light it. The children plodded wearily after the tireless Dweorg. They were ready to drop by the time they reached the top. Dringol halted. To their dismay they saw by the light of his torch no more than a short upward sloping tunnel that led to a dead end.

Peter gathered himself to protest when the Dweorg pointed his staff. To their immense relief a stone rolled back to reveal a starlit sky and the cold snow shining beneath its light. Chill air blew upon them but it did not matter. Anything to be out of this hateful mountain and away from the wily Dweorg.

'Thank you for leading us,' said Peter. 'If you'll just show us which is the path, we'll be on our way.'

The Dweorg suddenly barred their way with his staff. His lip curled in an evil leer.

'Not so fast, if you please. I do not feel satisfied for my labours. Nor do I believe you have told me all you should. So I have one more riddle for you. And this time you shall answer first. If you are wrong or cannot answer, I shall keep the golden-haired ones.' He pointed to the girls. 'If you guess correctly . . . then we shall speak of what you might pay me for the last part of this journey. Now here is my riddle.

> 'Where meets the starlight
> And the stone?
> Who bears the birthright
> To her throne?'

Peter knew the game was up. Whatever answer they gave would betray Princess Alena. Without a moment's thought he rushed at the Dweorg as hard as he could and dived for his legs. The unexpected move caught the Dweorg off balance and gave the children their only chance.

'Quick, run for it. Run for your lives!' Peter cried as he scrambled to his feet and leapt towards the exit.

The others needed no second bidding. Andrew sprinted after his brother, followed closely by Sarah and Princess Alena, while the Dweorg bellowed with rage as they slipped round him. Peter darted into the open air and at once found himself slithering on frozen snow. He grasped frantically at an exposed rock and clung on for dear life. To his horror he saw that the cave came out halfway down a steep icy slope that ended not far below in a sheer precipice.

Meanwhile, inside the tunnel Dringol recovered him-

self with a howl of fury. Springing up, he pointed his
staff at the exit and muttered a spell that sounded like a
rumble of thunder. The rock began to close. Desperately,
Andrew dived through the narrowing gap to freedom.
But Sarah was not so fortunate. In her haste she stumbled and by the time she regained her footing it was too
late. She and the princess were trapped. With a cry of
despair she threw herself against the sealed rock.

Andrew was in even greater trouble. He landed on his
front and before he could even begin to collect his wits
he began to slide spread-eagled down the slope. Peter
watched horrified as he saw his brother slithering head-
first towards the edge of the precipice.

'Dig your feet in, Andrew,' he shrieked.

With agonising slowness Andrew came to an uncer-
tain standstill and lay helplessly splayed out on the
frozen snow, only metres from the drop.

'Pete, I'm stuck,' he gasped. 'What are we going to
do? I'm really scared.'

Peter looked frantically around him. How could he
reach his brother? He couldn't even move safely himself. If only he had a rope or something. Then the cold
began to bite into his body. His teeth chattered and
panic started to well up in his heart.

'Pete! Pete, I'm slipping again,' Andrew cried in terror. 'I can't stop myself.'

15

The Ice Maiden

Peter looked around desperately for help and it was only as he realised there was none that he looked up to the heavens. And there he saw the bright star, Elrilion. Unbidden, a strange cry came to his lips and he felt a hot shiver rush through him, like nothing he had ever experienced before.

'Eko Elmesh e kala yento coella.'

At first, nothing changed. Andrew continued to slide slowly towards the brink of death. Then something began to shimmer to Peter's left. A pillar of ice to which he had given no attention was glowing from within. The light grew brighter and brighter until his eyes could bear it no more and he was forced to turn his head away.

When he dared to look again, to his amazement there stood in the place of the pillar a lady – tall, pale and fair as the starlight. Yet she was not cold; from where he clung so desperately to the rock Peter felt a warmth that cheered his heart. The lady smiled.

He pointed to his brother. With a nod of understanding she made a smooth gesture with her hand that brought Andrew to an immediate halt. Then she strode with ease across that impossible icy slope to where Andrew lay sprawled little more than a metre from the edge. Her long white robe flowed gracefully as she went.

Stooping, she took Andrew by the hand and helped him to his feet. To his astonishment, Andrew found he could stand and walk without difficulty while holding her arm. Peter looked on with a mixture of joy, wonder and relief as they came towards him.

'Thank you. Thank you so much,' he cried, and there were tears in his eyes.

Silently she took his hand and led them both up the slope until they were on level ground and could stand unaided. Peter and Andrew felt overawed by her presence and hardly knew what to say.

'Thank you for rescuing me,' said Andrew.

'Who are you?' Peter asked.

'I am the Ice Maiden,' she replied. Her voice was soft and sweet. 'I came in answer to your cry.'

'I don't know what I said,' Peter stammered.

'Sounded like a foreign language to me,' Andrew said.

The Ice Maiden smiled. 'It was not foreign to my ears. That is sufficient.' Her eyes sparkled with the starlight. 'Now tell me, what brought you to such a plight?'

'The girls!' gasped Peter. 'They never escaped in time. That evil Dweorg has got them.'

Words tumbling from their lips, they told her all that had happened to them since they had met Dringol. The Ice Maiden listened patiently.

'The mountains are harsh and their laws stern.' She spoke gravely. 'Pray your companions have the heart to resist this Dweorg.'

'Sarah will be all right,' said Andrew. 'It's Alena I'm worried about.'

'Then I will give some aid to break the spell. It will

take a little time. Wish them well while I divine the way.'

* * *

In the dimly lit tunnel the girls shrank back against the wall as Dringol advanced on them. He gave a booming laugh.

'Ah, foolish ones! It has worked better than I planned, for it is one of you two who has what I desire,' he gloated.

'Don't you dare come any nearer,' Sarah screamed. 'You horrible, hateful beast!'

'And how will you stop me?' he taunted.

He stood a little more than two metres from where they cringed, and folded his arms.

'It's all right, Sarah,' whispered Alena. 'He can't take it from me by force. I'll be safe.'

'That doesn't help me much, does it?' Sarah replied, giving her a sharp glance.

'Let me have the Star Stone and then you shall go free,' the Dweorg demanded.

Slowly, Princess Alena removed it from her blouse. The Dweorg took a step forward.

'Stay where you are,' she ordered. 'I will not let you come closer.'

The Star Stone began to glow with a vivid blue intensity that lit up the tunnel.

Dringol laughed, but the moment he tried to take another step he found he could not do so. An invisible barrier had fallen between him and the girls. He pushed and shoved, then angrily muttered spells, but nothing worked.

'Well done!' cried Sarah.

Princess Alena looked rather pleased with herself and giggled as the Dweorg raged and fumed before them.

It was some time before his fury subsided and then a cunning gleam came into his eye. He sat down cross-legged and gazed at them.

'Well, well. Now you are in a fine pickle,' he said. 'I cannot reach you and you cannot reach your companions. Between us we have made a neat prison for you, have we not? All I need to do is to wait until hunger and thirst combine to break your wills. So, when you are ready, place the jewel on the floor in front of you, and we'll consider the matter at an end.'

The girls turned to one another in dismay. Actually, they were very hungry and especially thirsty. Just thinking about it made things worse. Dringol knew this and with a smirk on his face took a long swig from a flask that he carried in his belt.

For perhaps ten minutes nothing more happened. Dringol remained seated on the floor and the two girls stood with their backs to the sealed rock. No one spoke and a thick silence hung over the tunnel. Suddenly the Dweorg cocked his head to one side.

'Ah, I hear something. The sound of others coming from afar. Yet not so very distant, I judge.' He regarded the girls with a mocking stare. 'We have visitors. I think you may be acquainted with them.'

Sarah and the princess said nothing but both realised that it must be their pursuers. To remain trapped like this would be disastrous. Gublak might well possess powers to break the spell of the Star Stone. And he would show no mercy, least of all towards Sarah. What should they do?

Dringol guessed what was going on in their minds.

'Give me the jewel and you may go free,' he said. 'You still have time to escape. If not, I shall lead your hunters to their quarry.'

Princess Alena began to sob. 'We can't escape either way now. We've lost. I told you I shouldn't have come with you.'

'Don't give up,' said Sarah. 'We're not finished yet.'

But the princess had been through enough. The voices jabbered in her head and she began to tremble uncontrollably. Her eyes became wild and staring. She shrank from Sarah and bared her teeth. Her voice changed as she spoke, one moment harsh and demanding, the next weak and pleading.

'I am Princess Alena. I will rule with Gublak. Fetch him to me . . . No, don't please. I'm afraid. I'm not a princess . . . just an orphan, nobody . . . Don't touch me. I can destroy you. Bring me gold. I desire wealth. . . . No, I want to go home. I feel trapped, so helpless. . . . Gublak is my friend, my hope . . . No, he's a liar . . .'

Sarah was aghast as she watched the princess go to pieces. She didn't know what to do. When she tried to reach out her arms in comfort the princess merely knocked them away. The Star Stone began to fade. Dringol rubbed his stubby hands together with anticipation.

'Aha, now I have you,' he gloated. 'Give it to me.'

'Y . . . yes, t . . . take it,' said the princess through

chattering teeth. 'It's of no use.'

'No, Alena, don't!' cried Sarah. Suddenly remembering, she reached into her jerkin and drew out the second of the three feathers given to her by the turtle dove.

The princess ignored her and reached behind her neck to release the clasp. Dringol's eyes gleamed.

Sarah leapt forward and stood between the princess and the Dweorg. The feather shone like a silver dagger in her hand. 'I won't let her give it to you,' she said. 'You'll have to get past me first.' She jabbed the feather menacingly at the Dweorg. 'Get back. Go on,' she cried.

By now the Dweorg was angry and his hand reached for his fearsome axe.

'Alena, pull yourself together,' Sarah snapped. 'I need your help.'

Dringol took a few steps back. Then he raised his axe over his head and with a cry of rage he charged with all his might at Sarah, intent on splitting her down the middle.

At that very moment, there was a deep rumble and the ground shook beneath their feet. The rock that blocked off the tunnel's exit began to crack and to crumble. Dringol stopped in his tracks and the two girls shrank back, wondering what was going on. The next instant, a blistering white light dazzled their eyes, blinding out everything. Dringol screeched in terror, turned on his heels, and promptly fled for his life, leaving the two girls cowering on the ground, dreading to look.

The noise and light slowly faded until all was still. They waited in apprehension. Then, to their surprise and delight, they heard Peter's voice.

'Sarah, Alena. It's all right. You're safe!'

The two boys rushed in and flung their arms around the girls. The Ice Maiden stood smiling at the tunnel entrance as the children whooped and danced with delight.

'Thank goodness you came,' Sarah gasped. 'You were only just in time, you know. But how on earth did you do it?'

Andrew grinned from ear to ear. 'We didn't,' he said. 'She did.'

For the first time Sarah and the princess noticed the Ice Maiden. Holding hands they slowly approached her.

'Whoever you are, thank you.' There was awe in Sarah's voice as she spoke. 'I wondered if there was any hope for us.'

'Things are only hopeless when there is no hope in the heart,' she said. 'Now, you must be Sarah. And you are Princess Alena.'

'She's the Ice Maiden,' said Andrew. 'She saved my life.'

Between them Peter and his brother explained how the Ice Maiden had appeared and rescued them after their escape from the cave. When they had reached the safety of level ground she had stood quietly singing to the stars before returning to the Dweorg's door. Then her whole being had begun to pulsate with light until the boys had to shield their eyes – and then the rock simply crumbled before her.

Sarah then told the three of them what had taken place in the tunnel.

The Ice Maiden looked at Princess Alena and spoke with understanding in her voice. 'Poor child,' she said to the still trembling girl. 'We must see what can be done.' She beckoned to the others. 'Come now and do not fear. Dringol will not dare return yet.'

'What about Gublak and his wolves?' Peter asked.

She laughed. 'They will have a difficult journey to reach here. And though some may pass they shall pay dearly for their trouble.'

Together they stood at the entrance and looked out on the snowy mountain and the awesome slope that had so nearly claimed Andrew's life.

'I can't walk on that,' wailed the princess.

'Nor can I,' muttered Sarah.

'Don't worry. It's quite safe. You watch,' Andrew reassured them.

A pink glow seemed to radiate from the Ice Maiden and in its aura the children felt warm and secure. The girls found to their astonishment that they could walk with just as much ease on the treacherous ice as they could on dry ground.

The Ice Maiden led them up the slope until they came to a cave carved into solid blue-green ice. They were invited to enter. The sight that met their eyes was magical. Before them lay a huge cavern of brightly lit ice. All the colours of the rainbow flashed and flickered around the crystalline walls. Great silvery icicles hung from the roof. Many-faceted geometric ice shapes covered the floor in dazzling splendour.

'Wow!' cried Andrew. 'Is this where you live?'

The Ice Maiden nodded, evidently pleased at their reaction. She guided them down a broad crystal stairway until they came to a small pool that lay green and still in the floor.

'This will sustain and refresh you,' she explained. She

took four crystal goblets and filled them from the pool.

The liquid was warm and sweet, and the moment they tasted it a thrill ran through their bodies. It was as she had said – after one goblet full, each felt as though they had eaten a three-course meal. Moments later drowsiness overtook them. Peter looked alarmed but the Ice Maiden laid a hand on his arm.

'Do not fear, Peter,' she whispered. 'You will rest only a short time before you resume your journey.'

She was so reassuring that he relaxed and was soon fast asleep. Andrew and Sarah likewise dozed off. Princess Alena made to lie down but the Ice Maiden restrained her.

'No, not you, Alena,' she said gently. 'Come with me, for we must speak and I would like to assist you.'

Together they walked back to the entrance and stood facing the stars. At the Ice Maiden's bidding Princess Alena told of all her adventures. When she had finished, the lady turned to her with a solemn look and then calmly lifted the silver chain and cupped the Star Stone in her hand. The princess drew back in sudden panic, fearful lest the Ice Maiden should be harmed or should snatch it from her.

'Do not worry, child,' she reassured her. 'It will not harm me, nor would I steal it, for it is yours alone. But you have yet to realise what it is you possess. Guard it well, for what you have treated as a trinket is so power-ful it could change an empire. Many would like to obtain it for that reason. Gublak has sought to seduce you into surrendering it. His greed is insatiable but it serves pur-poses even more evil. You must understand this.'

'But what does it matter?' cried the princess. 'I am

only an adopted child. How can this be called my birth-stone? It's a lie.'

The Ice Maiden released the jewel.

'Adopted you may be, yet to those who receive a gift such as this it is as though they had been born into the royal line from the first. Unnamed you were, but Star-born you became. This is truly your birthstone, Alena.' She emphasised the girl's name. 'Alena – if you relin-quish it through carelessness, greed or folly, all will be lost. Then you will become as nobody, and kingdoms will fall. You yourself would grow corrupt beyond your imaginings. Can you see what is at stake?'

Princess Alena nodded quietly. 'I understand only a little of what you say, but I do see that I have been very foolish and brought my companions and myself to great danger. What shall I do? I do not know my own mind any longer. Can you help me?' She gazed up at the Ice Maiden with pleading eyes.

'You and your friends must complete the journey,' she replied. 'I see your healing lies at its end. Yet I may bring you comfort in your trial and a great measure of relief. See the star, Elrilion? Gaze upon it and hold the Star Stone in your grasp. I will sing for you.'

Princess Alena did as she was told and the Ice Maiden started to sing. The song was like nothing the princess had ever heard before.

It began with a soothing hum that gently rose and fell like the sighing of the night wind in the trees. It took the princess in memory back to when she lay in her mother's arms and heard her sing a lullaby.

The song broke into the merry chatter of birds as they greet the dawn. Laughter filled the princess's heart and she remembered her childhood playmates. The Star Stone felt warm in her hand.

The Ice Maiden threw back her head and a triumphant melody resounded through the crags and valleys. It was like the rising sun conquering the remains of night and blazing over the eastern horizon. The Star Stone burned hot in the princess's grasp and she loved her father.

Then the melody died away to be replaced by a high, silvery song of crystal clarity. Princess Alena knew she was hearing the long-lost echoes of the music of the stars at the dawning of time. It was strange, magical and unearthly. She stood mesmerised. Tears rolled down her cheeks. In the back of her mind she heard the chatter of those mad voices but the sound was receding like a noisy crowd passing into the distance. Her head felt fresh and clear.

How long the song lasted or when it ended she could not say. It was only when the Ice Maiden spoke that she again became aware of her surroundings.

'Come, Alena. It is done. Now we must wake your friends, for this night passes.'

The princess smiled and carefully replaced the Star Stone inside her blouse. 'Thank you,' she said simply.

It did not take long to rouse the others, all of whom felt as if they had slept for days. The princess, too, felt refreshed but neither she nor the Ice Maiden spoke of what had happened.

Accompanied by the Ice Maiden, they left the cave. She led them across the ridge and they began their descent on the other side, just as the first pale hint of dawn was tingeing the eastern sky.

Before long, they could see their way. The pass down which they travelled ran right to the valley floor and soon they reached the line where the snow gave way to heather. Here the Ice Maiden stopped.

'Now I must leave you,' she explained. 'Elmesh go with you and give you courage.'

'Thank you so much for helping us,' said Peter. 'We would never have made it without you.'

'Oh, but we don't even know your name,' exclaimed Sarah.

For a brief instant the beautiful face of the Ice Maiden clouded. 'It is decreed that I cannot tell my name, except to him I shall one day love. Nor can I go farther until that time shall come – whenever it may be,' she sighed.

There was an awkward silence that Andrew broke with his customary cheerfulness. 'Oh well, I'm sure it'll come soon,' he said. 'Then you can tell us all about it.'

She smiled. 'One last thing: you still have far to go and perhaps dangers to face. This will help you should you need it.' She drew from her robe a large crystal and passed it to Peter. 'It will not melt while your heart is strong. Carry it well for it is destined to accomplish much more than your protection alone.'

Peter thanked her and put it in his pocket.

'Farewell,' she cried and the next instant she vanished from their sight.

The four companions turned towards the rising sun and began their descent into the green valley below.

16

Flip-flop

It was a happy party that wove down the mountainside, and all four chattered non-stop about their exciting adventures.

'I really thought I was a goner,' said Andrew.

'*You* did? You should have been in the tunnel with us,' Sarah retorted. 'It was scary! Especially when we thought Gublak was coming after us as well.'

She had decided to say nothing about Princess Alena's panic but the princess spoke up for herself. 'I'm sorry for the way I behaved. I just lost it. It all suddenly seemed too much for me to cope with.'

'Oh, that's all right,' Sarah replied. 'It's over now.'

'Are you really feeling better?' Peter asked the princess.

'Yes, much,' she answered. 'The Ice Maiden helped me when you were asleep.'

Everyone thought the Ice Maiden was marvellous and hoped they would meet her again sometime. Sarah had some ideas of her own about that.

The air grew warmer as they descended and it promised to be a sunny day. A fine haze hung over the rolling landscape that stretched out before them. It felt good to be alive and for the moment they forgot all about their enemies.

Which was why, perhaps, they failed to notice a black speck hovering high above them.

* * *

Gublak's fury knew no bounds when he discovered the children's escape through the whirlpool. He roared and raged at the top of his voice, then he sent Urgils and wolves scurrying all over the island to track them down, with promises of vast rewards to whoever caught them.

Greed for the Star Stone consumed him. It had been so nearly within his grasp and now the desire for it burned like a fever within his body. He would do anything, pay any price, to obtain it. A kind of madness took hold of him.

'I must have it. I will have it. No one will stop me. It's mine. All mine. I will have it. I will have it,' he muttered as he paced up and down the corridors of his fortress.

When Crow came winging back with the news that the children had escaped to the mainland he made up his mind to follow at once. Gathering all his guards and the whole wolf pack he boarded the pirate ship and ordered the captain to make for the cove. The pirates, who lived in fear of Gublak and his forces, did everything they could to speed the ship on its way. There was no knowing what he might do.

Yet even in his madness Gublak planned carefully. With the aid of the longboat, he landed only Ulris and his wolves on the beach, instructing them to hunt the children down and lead them captive across the mountain to the plains below.

He and his Urgils, meanwhile, set sail southwards and rounded the mountainous headland known as Illian Head. By sunrise the following morning *Grimwolf* had anchored just offshore where the land ran down to a beach. The crew set about landing the provisions and horses and weapons that they had hurriedly loaded onto the ship.

'Do you want us to wait 'ere, yer Eminence?' asked Captain Gaspar.

'No,' said Gublak. 'You are all coming with me. I want every man and beast you have to join in the search. They must be recaptured at all costs. Do you understand?'

'Aye, aye, sir,' the captain replied. 'But the men won't like it.'

Gublak glared at him. 'Tell them, Captain, that I will deal personally with any who complain. And remind them that I reward loyal servants well.'

So, a large party of Urgils and pirates, some on horseback along with Gublak, began to head northwards to meet the wolves. If the children escaped Ulris they would not outwit Gublak a second time. He would see to that.

Meanwhile, Ulris and his wolves had fared badly. Following the same trail up the mountain as the children, they reached the Slabs of Dringol by the early evening of the previous day. There they lost the scent and although they spent a long time scouting around for tracks, in the end they had to admit to having no idea which direction their quarry had taken. By then it was dark. Aside from calling off the search, there was only one other option. Ulris made the decision to cross the mountain by way of the high snow-covered ridge ahead.

It was to prove costly, for the Ice Maiden was true to her word. A freak storm blew up from the north and before long the wolves were battling with all their might against a fierce blizzard.

'This is strange work,' Ulris growled. 'Some powerful force is opposing our hunt.' Baring his fangs, he grew more determined than ever and urged the pack on.

But the weather drove the pack steadily southwards so that they missed the ridge and were forced down another valley instead. Many of the wolves died in the storm and a grim-faced Ulris vowed vengeance.

By dawn, the pack, still struggling through the snow, was reduced to no more than thirty strong. They had crossed the mountains but were now far to the south of the children.

It was then that they caught sight of Crow.

* * *

Oswain dreamed that night. At first he saw a whirl of spinning lights, then they began to slow and he saw that each was a bright ball that had a line attached to it. Some invisible hand far away was making them spin. A light flashed and a silver feather appeared, slicing through the strings and allowing the shining globes to fly apart. Then from what he knew to be the east he heard a voice calling, calling him home to Alamore. It was the voice of Trotter.

When he woke, Oswain glanced across at Brankleshanks. They had slept under the stars and the Dweorg was snoring loudly. Oswain rose and stretched. His dream was a sign, of that he was certain, but what did it mean? He pondered for a long time and then it came to him – everyone was being pulled by the Star Stone: Gublak, Brankleshanks, probably Dringol, Oswain himself and the mice. Yet what really mattered was Alena herself, with or without the Star Stone. He realised that he was being led astray. It would be a big risk but he knew now what to do.

'Come on, Brankleshanks. It's time we were on the move.' He stirred the Dweorg with his foot and the Dweorg was none too pleased.

'It's still dark,' he grunted. 'Go away.'

Oswain was insistent and he soon had Brankleshanks awake and mounted on his back.

'I'm changing direction,' he said, as he set off at a brisk pace.

'You can't do that. Why?' the Dweorg complained.

'I've had a dream. We are meant to go north-east, not south-east. We will find Alena and no doubt Gublak if we go this way.'

'What if you are wrong? Here, put me down and listen. My brother told us where we should go.'

'I don't trust you and I don't trust your brother, and I'm not wrong. So be quiet or I'll dump you right here!'

Just as he said those words, Oswain found himself on a long scree slope and with no hesitation launched himself into the slide, leaving his passenger to cling on for dear life as they descended a very rapid three hundred metres. There was no going back now, either for him or his passenger.

* * *

'I wish I knew where we were going,' Peter muttered.

The party had reached the lowlands and ahead of them stretched a landscape of open woodland and grassy moors. From the sun's position they knew which way was east, but that was about all.

'Do you know where we are, Alena?' Andrew asked.

She shook her head. 'Not really. My home city must be north across the mountains. And somewhere this side must be the Great Forest. . . .'

'The Great Forest! Then that's where we must make for,' Sarah cried. 'Oswain will be there. And he's bound to help us.'

Princess Alena looked dubious. She felt uncomfortable every time she thought about her stepbrother, wondering what he would say if they met, especially in view of all the trouble she had caused. Sarah noticed this.

'Look, I know how you feel, Alena, but it will be all right. I think he's wonderful and I'm sure he won't be cross with you. Anyway, I've had enough of crossing mountains for the moment.'

The others agreed that they must aim for the Great Forest, though nobody really knew what direction to take.

Just then they heard a strange noise coming from behind some bushes. It sounded something like,

'Nnnnughh! Phew!' They stopped and listened to this odd grunting, which was repeated several times over. Very cautiously, all four crept closer and peered through the undergrowth. The most unexpected sight met their eyes.

A large brown rabbit dressed in a blue top coat with a yellow waistcoat and sporting a red spotted bow-tie was busily heaving something out of the ground. For a moment they wondered what on earth he was up to. Then out popped a large juicy carrot. He mopped his brow with a handkerchief that matched his bow-tie.

Sarah tried to stifle a giggle. The rabbit pricked up his ears at the sound and they thought he would bolt, but instead he scratched his head and waddled in their direction. Peter was on his guard but he need not have worried.

'Oh, there you are,' exclaimed the rabbit as he rounded the bushes to where they crouched. 'I wondered where I might find you. Flip-flop's the name. Jolly pleased to meet you.'

He held out a paw which Peter shook awkwardly. 'Pleased to meet you, too,' he mumbled. The others did the same.

'Who are you?' Princess Alena demanded.

'I told you: Flip-flop. I've been sent to look for you and lead you to Trotter – well, volunteered, really. Felt they needed someone and thought I'd have a go.'

'You weren't doing much looking just then, were you?' said Andrew.

'Breakfast,' he replied. 'You know, the most delicious carrots grow in this part of the world. Best I've tasted since, oh, I don't know when.'

'We might have missed you altogether,' said Peter. 'Then what?'

'But you didn't,' the rabbit replied with an airy wave of his paw. 'Now how about breakfast? I for one am very hungry. Carrots anyone?'

'He's nuts!' whispered Andrew.

The others agreed.

Still, carrots were better than nothing and they joined Flip-flop in devouring the pile he had pulled up. Sarah had a fit of giggles as she listened to all the crunching sounds and stared at this ridiculous rabbit.

'Are you sure it was Trotter who sent you?' Peter queried. The rabbit did seem the most unlikely guide imaginable. But then he recalled Fumble, Mumble and Grumble, the three crazy mice who had helped them in their previous adventure. They hardly gave you confidence at first sight.

'Oh yes,' munched the rabbit. 'Well, more or less. Though I must be honest and say I haven't done a lot of this sort of thing before. Like I say, I volunteered. Love travelling. Seeing the sights and all that. Hope they realise I've gone. Forgot to tell anyone.'

'You're joking.'

'No.'

'Well, how far is it to the Great Forest?' demanded Andrew.

'How long is a healthy carrot?' Flip-flop returned. 'It depends if we stick to the main path or take the pretty route. I rather fancy the pretty one myself.'

'You do realise we're being followed, don't you?' said Princess Alena.

He raised a reassuring paw. 'Don't worry your pretty

little head, Princess. Too much worry is bad for the digestion. You'll be quite safe with me. Have another carrot.'

Delighted as they were to have someone who would lead them to Trotter, and hopefully to Oswain, too, the children really did begin to wonder what they were letting themselves in for. They soon discovered the reason for his name, too. The rabbit had simply enormous flat feet that made a flip-flopping sound as he waddled along with his white tail bobbing from side to side. The children found it difficult not to laugh.

They followed a path of sorts but every so often Flip-flop would stop dead and then run on ahead without a word of explanation. Thinking that he had spotted some danger the children kept diving for cover in the undergrowth. But each time, to their annoyance, he came back with a lettuce or a cabbage or another carrot. If that wasn't the reason, it was, as he explained to them, because he had seen 'something interesting'.

'This is getting ridiculous,' Peter declared. On this occasion they had left the obvious route and were stumbling through brambles and tussocks of long grass. 'Hey, Flip-flop, can't we keep to the path?'

'What's that?' cried the rabbit. 'This is much more fun. Don't like paths much. Where's your sense of adventure?'

'I think I've had quite enough adventure for the moment,' Peter muttered as he unhooked himself from yet another bramble.

The next instant they heard an 'Oo! Ouch! Ah!' and Flip-flop vanished from their sight. They looked around in vain until a groan told them where he was. All four stumbled across to find the rabbit lying on the ground with his paws waving in the air.

'Ah, there you are,' he gasped. 'Help me up, will you?'

'What happened? Are you all right?' Andrew asked.

'Oh yes, silly me. I tripped over a rabbit hole,' he replied.

'How on earth can a rabbit trip over a rabbit hole?' Sarah exclaimed.

'Oh, I do it all the time,' he explained. 'Someone always leaves them in the wrong place.' He shouted down the hole. 'Anyone at home? No? Oh well, thought not.'

'That will teach you to keep to the path,' said Princess Alena. But, of course, it didn't, and they spent the whole day like this, stopping every so often to eat yet more of the vegetables that Flip-flop found, or to pick him up from yet another fall. If they were not doing that, it was pulling him out of the mud or trying to find the path after he had lost it.

On one occasion they found him stuck upside down in a hole with only his hind legs waving in the air because he had overbalanced and fallen in head first while shouting 'Hello'. They nearly split their sides laughing before they pulled him out.

But as the evening drew on they all began to tire.

'Phew, can we stop soon?' Peter asked.

'Not yet,' Flip-flop replied. 'Not here.'

'Why not?'

'No breakfast.'

'Blow breakfast,' Andrew retorted. 'My legs ache. I want to rest.'

The rabbit halted.

'Tell you what, I know a short cut to breakfast from here.'

'Oh no, not again!' they chorused.

'What do you mean, "breakfast"?' Sarah asked.

'Carrots, of course. It's no use waking up without carrots, is it? Anyway, I like sleeping in a carrot bed.'

The others groaned.

'You and your stomach!' said Andrew.

However, in spite of their tiredness and misgivings the children agreed to take the short cut to where the carrots grew.

It was one of the worst decisions they ever could have made. Especially as Crow spied their path from high above.

* * *

Later that evening, not so very far to the south-west, Gublak and Ulris met and made camp in a stone hollow. The news from Crow was received with the greatest of interest.

17

Treachery Uncovered

Dringol was furious. Just when the Star Stone was within his grasp he had been thwarted and he didn't know by whom. Yet whoever it was possessed a power far greater than his own and he fled for his life, running to the very bottom of his tunnels until, as dawn broke, he emerged eastwards onto the lower slopes of the mountains, though in a valley to the south of the children.

Snow had fallen in the night and it stretched in a white sheet broken only by the dark crags of Cadaelin. Though the weather eastwards was sunny, the peaks were still shrouded in ominous clouds. Dringol gazed about him, and then he spied a dark shape lying in the snow. Plodding across he came upon the corpse of a dead wolf. Not far away he saw another. Realisation creased his features. If the wolves had come this way then so presumably had the children. Maybe it wasn't too late to catch them after all.

Grunting with satisfaction, he set off eastwards as fast as he could.

* * *

Moving with equal haste from a more southerly direction Oswain and Brankleshanks came upon the same snow fields.

'Is this what you saw in your dream, Oswain?' Brankleshanks demanded.

'No, it wasn't.'

'So do you think you can really carry me across that without breaking both our necks?'

'We'll just have to try, won't we?' Oswain answered. 'But if any necks are going to be broken, I'll make sure it's yours first!'

Oswain was thoroughly fed up. He wondered how much farther he must carry his annoying burden, and in how many more directions. What was the point of it all, he wondered? As for Grumble, he was either lost or dead – and Oswain still hadn't found the princess.

In this frame of mind he ploughed on into the snow, hoping that before too long they would reach lower ground and be clear of it.

'What's that over there?' Brankleshanks was waving with his finger at a line of markings in the snow to their left.

'It looks like tracks of some kind.'

'Take a look.'

Resisting the impulse to drop Brankleshanks there and then, Oswain obeyed.

The tracks proved to be a long line of footprints that swept over the rise and up into the mountains in one direction and down the slope into the other.

'Wolf prints,' Oswain muttered.

'Gublak!' exclaimed Brankleshanks. 'I begrudge you this, but you were right, Oswain of Alamore. We've picked up the trail. Though I don't relish the wolves,' he added.

'Strange that your brother should have sent us in a different direction,' Oswain observed.

'Never mind, never mind. Let's be after them.' The Dweorg was excited and fingered his axe.

The trail led them down a steep bend that swept around a large crag. Oswain gazed out across the Waste Plains ahead. To his relief there was no further sign of snow and the sun was up.

They had just reached the bottom of the slope and the edge of the snow when Oswain stopped for a breather. Brankleshanks slipped from the harness to stretch his legs. Suddenly there was a movement to their right and the sound of a whimpering snarl. Both whirled round to find themselves confronted by a slavering wolf. Brankleshanks' hand flashed for his crossbow and in seconds he had the creature in his sights.

'Hold off,' cautioned Oswain. 'He's in a bad way. Don't shoot unless he attacks.'

He addressed the wolf: 'Are you with Gublak the goblin?'

'Do I look as though I'm with anyone,' the wolf snarled.

'Then what are you doing here and where is your pack?' Oswain demanded.

'Pah! The pack has left me and many more like me to die,' the wolf answered, breathing in heavy gasps. 'We should have turned back when the storm came but our leader drove us on. It was terrible, even for a wolf.'

'What was your urgency?' Brankleshanks asked.

'Huh, some princess and some children. They are not worth the deaths of my kinswolves.'

Oswain and Brankleshanks looked at each other.

'But no Gublak?' Oswain queried.

'No, he will travel an easier route. I care nothing for him now,' said the wolf, gasping and coughing.

'Then let me help you,' Oswain offered, but before he could move there was a sudden sound like an angry hornet and the next instant the wolf lay dead with a crossbow bolt sticking from its heart. Oswain whirled on Brankleshanks, his face furious. 'I thought I told you not to shoot,' he shouted.

But Brankleshanks had not moved and the bolt was still in his bow.

The mystery was solved moments later when a stocky figure emerged from behind a rock.

'Dringol!' Brankleshanks gasped. 'What are you doing here?'

'Saving your lives, by the looks of it,' the Dweorg replied. 'This I take it is Oswain. But why are you so far off course? The princess is surely in the south with Gublak.'

'No, she is not,' said Oswain quietly. 'And nor was she ever. Brankleshanks, your brother has deceived you.'

Brankleshanks stood stock still for a moment. The pain in his leg, the fruitlessness of his search and the frustration of not having his heart's desire welled up within him. He turned on his brother as the truth dawned.

'You wanted the Star Stone for yourself, didn't you?' he snarled. 'You were planning to cheat me, you swine! I bet you just wanted me out of the way.'

Dringol made no pretence. 'What of it?' he snapped. 'I've worked hard for you. What reward would I have got? You get your revenge. You get the Star Stone, and I get – nothing!'

'I expected some loyalty from my own brother,' Brankleshanks yelled. 'After all I've been through . . .'

'Don't think I haven't suffered,' cried Dringol. 'I was nearly killed last night by a power too terrible for words because of you. Driven from my own home, I was.'

'It's the least you deserve, you greedy toad,' retorted Brankleshanks.

Oswain's mind was racing. So, Brankleshanks had wanted the Star Stone for himself. He had wondered about that. Then what had he done with Grumble? As for Dringol . . .

'Silence!' he cried. 'I am the one who has been most deceived. You have led me on a wild goose chase through the mountains, both of you, and you have put the life of my sister in serious jeopardy. Now, before we do anything else, what has happened to my companion, Grumble?'

Brankleshanks was fuming but silent.

'I'll tell you,' said Dringol. 'He shot him. Took him prisoner as a guarantee that you would give him the Star Stone when you found your sister.' He eyed his brother. 'He calls me greedy, but he wants everything!'

'So now we have a problem,' Brankleshanks growled. 'Three of us want the Star Stone but only one of us can have it.' He smirked. 'Yet I still hold the cards. If you want to see your companion Grumble alive again, Oswain, you will carry me until we find your sister.'

'But I want you dead, Oswain,' said Dringol. 'For then my brother is helpless and I can make my own pursuit.' He reached for a fresh bolt for his crossbow, but before he could so much as load it Brankleshanks pulled the trigger on his own crossbow and let fly with a deadly bolt.

The arrow struck Dringol in the thigh and knocked him to the ground. Howling and writhing with pain he clutched his wounded leg where he had fallen.

'Now see what it feels like to be crippled!' Brankleshanks yelled, clearly mad with rage.

Oswain was appalled but seized his chance and in a flash moved fast to disarm both brothers of their weapons, knocking Brankleshanks hard to the ground in the process.

'I should walk away from both of you,' he said hotly. 'Between you, you have betrayed me and my family and my friends. Perhaps I should leave you to the mercy of the wolves and the elements. In fact, you should thank Elmesh that I don't kill you here and now.' He clapped his hands to his head. 'Why did I ever listen to you?' He rounded on the Dweorgs where they lay. 'You had better tell the whole story, both of you, and I want no lies. Do you understand?'

So out came the treachery of the Dweorgs, both against Oswain and against each other – everything from their use of a hawk to intercept the message from Elmar, to Dringol's encounter with the children.

When they had finished Oswain nodded. 'I cannot understand how these children are involved but at least Alena is alive. Yet if what you say is true then the wolves and Gublak may be upon them. I can't delay any longer. Goodbye, and consider well the fruits of your greed.'

Both Dweorgs looked up at him in anguish as the

seriousness of their plight hit them.

'We have been fools,' gasped Dringol. 'And now we are both doomed.'

'The wolves will return and avenge their dead on us,' Brankleshanks groaned. 'I am sorry, my brother.'

'And I, too,' Dringol agreed.

They turned to Oswain as he gathered up their weapons. 'Will you not have mercy and help us?'

Oswain was so angry that everything in him wanted to be on his way and to leave the evil Dweorgs to their fate, but something checked him. In spite of himself, he felt an unexpected rush of compassion for the now helpless brothers. He couldn't just leave them.

'I don't know if I can. Certainly Elmesh knows I cannot carry you both. Perhaps he will be merciful in some way. All I know is that you must give up your desire for the Star Stone.' He shook his head. 'Such greed is a terrible thing. You cared nothing for my sister but only for what she possessed. Yet neither you nor Gublak would be happy in having it for yourselves. You would want more, but each gain would satisfy you less until you became slaves to your desires and possessions. It is an evil path to tread.'

'What can we do?'

Remembering something of Dweorg lore, Oswain decided to take a risk.

'You must renounce this greed on the life of the mother who bore you,' he said.

There was a silence for some moments.

'That would be for us one of the deep oaths, binding for all time. We could not make it lightly and we would become your servants for life,' said Dringol.

'True, but you must make it speedily for I must save the life of my sister,' Oswain answered.

And so, on the snow covered slopes of Cadaelin, Dringol and Brankleshanks swore their oath and far above, as though somehow seen and heard, a white light blazed from one special peak. Oswain saw it and, scarcely knowing what he was doing, he placed a hand on the leg of Brankleshanks and to his amazement felt it straighten. With his eyes still fixed on the light, he did the same for Dringol. At once the bolt eased from the wound and the flesh closed up with only the smallest of scars.

Oswain gasped. 'I have never before had within my gift as king the skill to heal,' he said. 'Some strange grace is at work that surely only Elmesh knows.'

Both Dweorgs rose to their feet amazed. Brankleshanks had tears in his eyes. 'I never thought I'd be free of my disability,' he breathed. 'Yet I can walk with ease.' He began to leap and run and laugh through the tears of joy that poured down his gnarled face.

'For my part, I expected to die, yet my life is spared,' exclaimed Dringol.

Then the two brothers embraced each other and solemnly put an end to their wrongs.

Oswain, with a smile on his lips, gazed up at the mountain peak. 'Thank you, whoever you are,' he whispered. 'Now perhaps I know why I was sent on this strange journey. I see, too, that mercy must be in the heart before healing can take place.'

'Our oath is secure and our legs are strong. We will go with you, Oswain,' Dringol declared.

'Aye,' agreed Brankleshanks.

'Then let us go, and quickly,' cried Oswain. And with that they were off as fast as their six healthy legs could carry them.

* * *

'What a commotion! What a commotion!'

Mrs Trotter bustled to the front door of her cottage wiping her hands on her apron as she did so. The mouth-watering smell of fresh baked bread filled the air. 'Mind you leave it to cool,' she called to her husband as she lifted the latch.

Before her stood two dusty mice looking utterly exhausted and gasping for breath.

'Quick, where's Trotter?' gasped one of them. 'It's urgent.'

The other gabbled something that made no sense at all and Mrs Trotter was just about to call her husband when he came into the passageway.

'Fumble! Mumble! You bring news and, by the looks of it, not good news?' the badger queried. 'Come in at once and tell us what you know.'

As soon as they were in Trotter's lounge the two mice blurted out their story of how Oswain had been duped into going in the wrong direction and of how Grumble had been shot.

'Where is Oswain now?' Trotter asked.

'Wedonnow,' said Fumble. 'Ecudbeanywer.'

'We need Stiggle. I'll have Foxy fetch him,' Trotter

decided. He rang a bell and a fox emerged from the next room. Trotter gave him his instructions and he shot off at once.

Just then Mrs Trotter came in carrying fresh bread and butter and jam. 'You must be famished,' she said. 'What a good job it's my baking day.'

'Thank you,' said Fumble. 'We've not eaten for at least a day. We're starving.'

'Well, help yourselves, m'dears,' said Mrs Trotter.

'Yumyum, inmytum,' said Mumble with a furry grin.

Stiggle arrived and quickly caught up on the news from the mice. 'This is serious,' he said. 'We already know that the princess is on her way here and, believe it or not, she's with Peter, Sarah and Andrew. Elmesh must have sent them again.'

'How did you find out?' asked Fumble.

Trotter looked grim. 'Three days ago a turtle dove arrived here. Or rather fell out of the sky, for the poor thing was as good as dead. It landed among some of the baby animals who were playing down by the ford and gasped out some dying words about the children, and that was it.

'The youngsters didn't come until yesterday and that was only because their parents had worked out that something was up. They told us as best they could but their story wasn't very clear,' Stiggle continued. He paused. 'Unfortunately, there was someone else with them – Flip-flop.'

'You're joking!' said Fumble. 'He's worse than all three of us mice put together!'

Trotter nodded. 'From what we can work out – and you can't blame the youngsters – Flip-flop took whatever message the bird was carrying and set off by himself to find the children and the princess without telling us. The trouble is we don't know which way he went.'

'I doubt if he does. He's all over the place. Too independent by far,' said Stiggle.

'I had hoped that Oswain might have found them all by now, but your news is grave,' Trotter sighed.

'Wecudgotoenchanedglad,' Mumble suggested.

'What? The Enchanted Glade? Oh, yes. We should do so at once. We need some guidance, I think.' The badger heaved another sigh. 'Somehow, I sense trouble ahead for all of us.'

18

The Earth-Trog

Squelch!

Peter groaned as yet again his boot sank in the mud.

'Hey, Flip-flop, this ground's terribly boggy, you know.'

'Forgot to tell you that,' the rabbit replied. 'It's all right if you keep to the dry bits, though.'

'That's if we can find any dry bits,' Andrew called.

'I hope it isn't too far,' said Princess Alena. 'The sun is beginning to set.'

'Hm, and it looks as though it might turn foggy,' Sarah added. 'I just hope that daft rabbit knows where he's going, that's all.'

It was fairly easy for Flip-flop to walk on this soggy ground because of his big feet. The others found it much more difficult so he had to keep waiting while they caught up with him. Since he hadn't thought of this the short cut was taking far longer than he'd planned.

As the sun set behind them it cast long shadows over the uneven ground. The air grew cool and misty. Ahead loomed the dusky shapes of old gnarled trees. It was becoming very wet underfoot.

'I don't like the look of this,' Peter mumbled. 'Hey, wait a bit, Flip-flop. Don't go so fast.'

'I can't see him,' said Sarah. 'I think we've lost him among those trees.'

The next instant, Peter put a foot wrong and his left leg sank so far into the bog that water seeped over the top of his boot. The others had to pull him out.

'Yeuk! I'm soaked,' he complained. 'I've got a boot full of slime. Go and find Flip-flop, will you, while I empty this out? And tell him to wait.'

The other three continued into the mist, calling for Flip-flop while Peter removed his boot and drained it. The fog soon closed in around him and by the time he had his boot back on again it was difficult to see where he was. The gloom was gathering and all the shadowy trees began to look the same. Peter suddenly felt afraid.

* * *

The stone hollow where Gublak and Ulris camped that same evening was a place of ancient evil. Rumours of ghosts and ghouls, of meetings with earth-spirits, kept folk from straying into its shadowy depths. The sailors sat uneasily around a fire on the rim of the hollow. They would come no further and only fear of Gublak kept them from fleeing for their lives. Though the Urgils and the wolves had sidled closer in, the same sense of unease filled their hearts.

Such a place suited the goblin well.

Gublak's consuming desire for the Star Stone led him to the blackest reaches of the hollow, where the dark had a deathliness all of its own. His eyes burned green and in their light appeared many other pairs of pale eyes, hovering in the murk, though no bodies could be seen.

Ulris gazed intently through half-lidded eyes as his master began to weave a spell. The sound of endless mournful sighs haunted his ears and a chill wind whirled around him. His fur prickled. He heard the faint cry of the goblin calling upon nameless dark powers. Then it seemed he dissolved into a ghastly green mist that ebbed into the earth. The wolf sat still, mesmerised.

*   *   *

Peter stumbled through the thickening mist. He called to his companions but his voice sounded weak and muffled. He knew he must not panic and so he pinched himself hard. To run now would be disastrous. Slowly, he picked his way from tree to tree, clutching at the wet bark and trying to find a safe place for his feet. The swampy ground smelt foul and he felt heavy inside. This was a bad place to be.

He felt something move.

Suddenly, a slimy tentacle whipped out of the swamp and snapped itself around his ankle. He fell with a loud splash. Then the mire began to heave and Peter cried out in fear. He was being pulled towards a dark mound by some dreadful unseen force. He thrashed around in an effort to free himself, but it was no good. A dank hole loomed ahead and with a rush of water and slime he was sent careering into its mouth.

Slithering and sliding, he shot into the earth and moments later landed on his backside in a stinking pile of mud and leaves. With his heart thumping fit to burst he staggered to his feet and looked around. Above his head hung hundreds of hairy roots. He could see no sign of the way by which he had entered. Ahead lay a tunnel lit by a faint grey phosphorescence. He thought he heard a noise, perhaps a cry, from somewhere along its length.

Very cautiously he began to creep forwards. Roots brushed at his face like giant living cobwebs. It was extremely cold and he shivered in his wet clothes.

Not far ahead the tunnel curved to the right and, as Peter rounded the bend, he received a terrible shock. There, transfixed against the wall, hung Flip-flop, bound by dozens of roots that had wrapped themselves around his limbs. His eyes stared vacantly into space and Peter feared he must be dead. He tried to tear the roots away, but the more he pulled, the tighter they gripped with a horrid creaking sound. Choking with despair he staggered blindly on.

All at once, the tunnel opened out into a cave and there to his horror he found his brother and sister and Princess Alena. They, like Flip-flop, did not move. Yet no tree roots held them; instead, their bodies were fused to the grey rock and before his horrified gaze they were slowly turning to stone. Already their legs and backs were cruelly transformed. His companions seemed destined to become nothing more than stone gargoyles staring from the harsh rock.

Peter's limbs grew leaden. He found he could no longer move his feet. Surely the same terrible fate awaited him. Then he heard a deep sinister voice.

'I am the Earth-Trog, devourer of the lost. You shall be mine for ever and ever. None can escape my grasp.'

·Peter struggled with all his will. 'Well, you're not having me,' he cried defiantly.

The voice laughed, hollow and mocking. 'But I shall, for a bargain has been struck.'

'What bargain?'

'A certain goblin desires a certain jewel. For the price of your souls I have agreed to assist him. That is the bargain. Now that I have my spoil, he shall have his desire. You will become part of me. Resistance is useless.'

At that moment a green mist started to seep into the cavern. Peter stared aghast as it formed into a lurid emerald slime on the floor. Slowly it began to take on the familiar gruesome shape of Gublak. In wild panic Peter struggled and cried out.

Something in the back of his mind tried to speak through the terror – a clear, cool word: 'This will aid you should you need it.' He struggled to remember what it was but a sleepy cloud muffled his memory.

Then it came to him. His arms, though stiff, could still move. With a supreme effort of will he reached into his pocket and closed his fingers gratefully around the Ice Maiden's crystal. He struggled to draw it out.

All the while the spirit of Gublak grew and grew before him until it assumed monstrous proportions. Peter was scared out of his wits. He managed to hold up the crystal but his heart quailed. To his dismay it began to melt between his fingers. The evil eyes of Gublak leered at his plight while the stone-cold grip of the Earth-Trog tightened about his limbs.

'No!' he gasped. 'Elmesh help me!'

The crystal was by now no more than the size of a pea and all hope seemed lost. Peter made one last desperate effort to conquer his fear. He thought of Oswain and the forest-folk. He remembered Aldred the stoat who had fearlessly come to their aid at the cost of his own life. A shiver of awe ran through his limbs. He set his jaw, and light began to shine from the crystal.

Slowly the stiffness eased from his limbs as his courage returned. He held the crystal high between his thumb and forefinger. Its triumphant blaze filled the cave.

'Now we will see who is the stronger,' he cried. A mighty strength filled his heart and he imagined he was a knight of olden times. He felt invincible as he approached the spectre of Gublak.

'Go, I command you in the name of Elmesh! You shall not have your desire. Begone now!'

The green image wavered and the face contorted in hatred, but with a hiss it began to fade until before long Peter stood alone. He smiled, though his face was grim.

'Earth-Trog, whatever you are, you cannot keep your bargain. You are denied your prey. Release these captives, or I'll burn the very heart out of you.'

The Earth-Trog growled but did not obey.

The light from the crystal spattered red, and tongues of fire began to lick at the cavern walls. Hanging roots shrivelled and smouldered. The air grew hot. A loud roar echoed at last from the earth.

'Enough!'

Peter remained unrelenting. 'Set them free,' he commanded. 'I will not stop until you obey.'

The Earth-Trog gave in. To Peter's relief he saw his companions come back to life. But he did not yet run to comfort them, for his will was set upon holding the fearsome Earth-Trog in check.

'Release the rabbit,' he ordered.

Moments later, Flip-flop came stumbling into the cave to join his dazed companions. They clearly had no idea of what was going on and seemed not to recognise Peter.

'Your power is matched, and mastered,' he declared. 'You will open a way to the earth above.'

'It shall be, for the moment, it shall be,' the voice rumbled.

There was a thunderous crash and one wall of the cavern split open to reveal a slope that led to level grass and a clear night sky.

'Follow me,' Peter ordered the others. Then, by the light of the crystal, he led them all out to safety.

The earth shook and the rent closed. 'Vengeance!' was the last threatening word Peter heard from the Earth-Trog.

Through the trees and onto higher, drier ground Peter led his band until, at length, he called a halt. Only then did he return the crystal to his pocket, before sinking to the ground in an exhausted heap. The others, at that point, came to themselves and recognised him for who he was.

'W . . . what happened?' asked Sarah. 'I feel as though I've just had a terrible dream. I fell down a hole and began to turn into stone. Then a shining knight with a blazing sword came to rescue me. And . . . and here I am,' she ended lamely.

'I've had the same dream,' Princess Alena said quietly. 'Only I saw Gublak coming towards me to snatch the Star Stone. Then I, too, was rescued.' She felt anxiously for the jewel around her neck.

Andrew's experience was similar, while Flip-flop thought he had been buried alive and was turning into a carrot.

'What about you, Pete?' Andrew queried.

His brother gave a relieved laugh. 'Oh, something like yours, I suppose.' He was not sure whether to tell them everything or not. In fact, it all seemed a bit of a dream to him now that it was over.

'All I can say is, we've had a very close escape. You were not dreaming, any of you. We could easily have been killed in that swamp.' He gave Flip-flop a stern look. 'You know, you really are stupid not to have kept to the path. What would Oswain have said if you'd lost us all, eh? You're supposed to show us the way, not lead us into a mess.'

The rabbit looked suitably crestfallen. 'I'm sorry,' he said. 'I suppose I didn't think about the dangers. I was more interested in finding those carrots.'

'Well, mind you don't make the same mistake again,' Princess Alena reprimanded him.

He nodded glumly. Somehow carrots didn't seem quite so important now.

'Can we get some sleep now?' Andrew pleaded. 'I feel as though I'm turning to stone.'

Peter glanced at him sharply, but Andrew laughed, 'Oh no, don't worry. Just tired, that's all!'

Everyone relaxed and then they snuggled down together to snatch a few hours' sleep.

* * *

A tremor in the ground woke Andrew. He blinked and nudged the others. The sun was well up and the day looked promising.

'Wakey wakey, everyone. Come on.'

'Oh, shush,' groaned Sarah. 'You're so noisy in the mornings, Andrew.'

The others stirred.

Their yawns and stretches were cut short by another tremor. Sarah looked anxiously at her elder brother.

'What do you think that is, Peter?'

'I'm not sure,' he replied slowly. 'But we made a new enemy under the ground yesterday, and he's not very happy with us. Come on, everyone. We need to be on our way – and fast.'

19
Flight

All night long Ulris sat in that hideous hollow where the wraiths had their dwelling. Never once did he move, yet his bright yellow eyes were always alert, watching and waiting.

Dawn broke over the horizon and the blackness turned to a cold, shadowy grey. There, motionless on the ground, lay the form of his master. The wolf rose and loped towards him. Gublak stirred as though from a deep sleep.

Ulris gave him an enquiring look. 'Have you had good success, Eminence?' he asked.

'I have travelled the dark places of the earth and met with kindred spirits,' the Goblin muttered. 'Dark and deliciously foul my paths have been – but no, I have not had success.' He spat the words with anger. 'So nearly in my grasp they were, again so close was my desire, but they possessed some fearsome power that even I and the Earth-Trog together could not resist. I was forced into retreat.'

The wolf growled.

'If it were not for those accursed children the Star Stone would be mine by now,' Gublak continued. 'If only that fool of a captain had not brought them to me in the first place. He must pay dearly for his folly!'

'Then the quest is lost?' the wolf asked. 'Shall we kill

the captain now, before we return to the island, or after?'

'No,' screamed the goblin. 'Fool! We are not going back. I have not come this far to be thwarted at the last. We shall take up the chase. I must have that jewel. Do you not understand? I see nothing else in my dreams. I long for its power. What could I not do if I possessed it! And it is in the hands of a foolish girl who does not have the smallest inkling of its importance. Pah!'

'They cannot be far from the Great Forest,' Ulris protested. 'You know what that means, Eminence. We have no power in that place of enchantment.'

'Then we shall draw them out,' snarled Gublak. 'The captain and his crew shall be useful to that end. Then, when their blood is shed in battle, it will be a fitting reward for the trouble they have brought upon me.'

The wolf's eyes gleamed. 'We will take the girl?'

Gublak nodded. 'Together with our revenge upon those companions of hers. I shall see to it that their death is slow and painful.'

'I, too, shall avenge my dead,' growled Ulris. 'Yet what, Eminence, if the princess still refuses of her free will to give you the Star Stone? You cannot take it by force.'

'Then she must die,' said the goblin. His eyes blazed. 'If the Star Stone cannot be mine, then no one shall have it. I have bargained with dark powers to possess it or to destroy it. Whichever way, my reward will be great. Rouse them, Ulris. We march at once!'

* * *

Ominous rumblings from deep underground urged the little band on. Even Flip-flop took the threat seriously. In fact, the only time he stopped was when he spotted some carrots growing by the roadside. The earth tremors had to wait while he dealt with the serious business of breakfast!

The ground trembled beneath their feet.

'Keep moving, everyone,' Peter yelled. 'Come on, Flip-flop.'

Needing very little encouragement, they hastened up a long wooded hill.

'It's as though we've woken some sleeping underground giant,' Sarah panted.

'That's exactly what it is, I reckon,' Peter answered. He glanced behind him.

Andrew came jogging alongside. 'D'you think we're going to have an earthquake? You know – with the ground splitting open and swallowing us up, and all that? I keep getting ready to jump back. Or should I jump forwards?'

'Oh, be quiet, Andrew,' Peter snapped. 'This is no joke.' He turned round to where the princess was lagging behind. 'Come on, Alena. Get a move on.'

'I'm doing the best I can,' she panted. 'And I'll thank you to treat a princess with a little more respect!'

'At least she's calling herself a princess again,' said Sarah. 'I hope it lasts.'

'Hm, she's still got to meet Oswain,' Peter replied. 'She doesn't seem very keen on the idea.'

'I'm not surprised,' Sarah retorted. 'She's expecting to be told off by her big brother. I don't like that either!'

The party reached the brow of the hill and before

them stretched a vast sweeping valley. Rough grassland tumbled down in rolling slopes to the valley floor, where a sandy brown expanse took over. In the distance a silvery thread glinted in the sunshine.

'We've reached the Waste Plains,' Flip-flop explained. 'That's the River Wendle over there.'

'So that's the Great Forest beyond it?' Andrew pointed to the dark expanse that spread as far as the eye could see.

'That's right,' Flip-flop acknowledged. 'We're nearly home.'

Just then the ground gave a sickening heave. A nearby tree toppled with a crash of branches and the skyline seemed to shake. The five companions clung to one another for support and waited in trepidation until the tremor passed. Flip-flop clutched his stomach and wished he hadn't eaten so many carrots.

'That was a big one. It's getting worse,' said Peter. 'We must hurry. Come on, let's run down this stretch.'

They dashed down the hillside into what they hoped was the safety of the valley. Flip-flop went onto all fours and fairly flew past everyone else. On and on they ran until the hill was far behind.

'Hang on. I've got a stitch,' Sarah gasped. 'Do you think it's safe to stop for a moment?'

'I don't think it's going to be safe until we get across the river,' said Peter. 'But all right.'

'I'm dying of thirst,' panted Princess Alena. 'Is there any water around?'

'As a matter of fact,' said Flip-flop with the air of one who knows, 'there's a stream just a bit farther on.'

'Well, let's keep going until we reach it,' said Peter.

'We'll walk, OK?'

However, when they reached the spot where the stream should have been, to Flip-flop's consternation they found nothing but a dried-up bed of stones.

'Odd,' he said. 'There's always water here. I wonder where it's gone?'

'Perhaps somebody's drunk it all,' suggested Andrew. 'Oh well, we'll just have to go without, I suppose. At least the Wendle's got plenty of water in it – if we last that long.'

The sun blazed hot and the air was sultry. It was very quiet. Just occasionally faint rumblings could be heard in the distance. Nobody spoke much. It was enough just to keep going. Not a drop of water was to be found anywhere.

At length, after hours of weary tramping, they came to where the grassland ended. They found themselves at the edge of a sandy cliff that through centuries of rain and frost had crumbled back to form dun-coloured mud-flats that spread out a hundred metres below where they stood. Dirty streams, now dried up, had cut deep chasms across the barren landscape so that it looked like something from another planet.

'Wow! Talk about soil erosion,' said Andrew. 'This cliff must have been falling to pieces for years.'

'Can we get down it?' Princess Alena asked anxiously.

'Oh yes,' the rabbit replied. 'We'll get a bit dusty, that's all. Nothing to worry about.'

'What about the mud? Is it soft or what?' Peter queried.

'Not at this time of year. It's fairly dry and you can walk on it,' Flip-flop reassured him.

'You'd better be right this time,' Peter warned.

The party began a cautious descent down the shallowest part of the cliff that they could find. It was very slippery with nothing to grab on to, and by the time they had slithered to the bottom everyone was covered in brown dust.

Much to their relief, Flip-flop was right about the mud. It was quite firm, though squelchy in places, and although they had to jump the cracks they made good progress.

'Next stop the river,' said Peter more cheerfully. He was beginning to feel a sense of relief. 'I think we're out of trouble now,' he said.

He spoke too soon. A fearsome roar from behind made everyone spin round. The cliff down which they had so recently come seemed to explode before their eyes. They watched awe-struck as a vast surge of black mire erupted from its length, pouring towards them like a huge crashing tidal wave.

'It's the Earth-Trog's revenge,' cried Peter. 'We'll be swamped alive. Run for it. Run for your lives!'

Nobody needed a second bidding. Panic stricken, they fled for the safety of the river, urged on by the thundering roar of the flood that bore down upon them.

Suddenly, Andrew, who was in front, came teetering to a halt.

'There's the river,' he shouted. 'But we've got to get down this. Look!'

He stood on the brink of another small cliff. It would only take five minutes to descend it, but they didn't have five minutes.

'We'll never do it,' Sarah screamed as she and the

others joined him.

They looked back in horror at the relentless black wave that was pouring and splashing across the mud-flats towards them. There was nothing they could do to avoid it.

All seemed lost. Then at once the air was rent by a shrill screech. Everyone looked up. It was Sarah who first recognised what it was. A magnificent white eagle was winging towards them, and his speed was simply breathtaking.

'It's Arca!' she cried. 'Look! He's come to rescue us!'

Moments later the great bird streaked in to land. He didn't waste a moment.

'On my back,' he cawed. 'One at a time. Hurry now.'

'You first, Alena,' Peter ordered. She protested that it should be Sarah but Peter was firm. 'Look, don't argue. You're the one we're supposed to be rescuing. Now get on.'

He gave her an unceremonious shove and she clutched desperately at the eagle's neck as he at once took to the air. The others watched as the bird swooped low across the river and deposited the princess safely on the other side.

'Thank goodness for that,' sighed Peter. 'You next, Sarah. And don't you argue either.'

Sarah leapt astride the eagle and rubbed his head with affection. 'Just like old times,' she laughed as they took off.

He took Andrew and Flip-flop together on the next trip, holding the petrified rabbit in his beak. Peter anxiously hopped from one foot to the other. The surging swamp, over twice his height, was scarcely twenty metres away as Arca set out towards him.

It was surely too late. As the wave reached him it reared up and Peter saw it take on the vile form of some primeval swamp monster. Baleful eyes glared hatred and malice as the Earth-Trog prepared to crush him to death. Its great shadow blotted out the sky and the air filled with a sour stench.

But Arca flew under the towering wave even as it crashed down. Summoning all his strength and speed, the mighty eagle seized Peter in his powerful talons and whisked him away to safety in the nick of time. The black mass spent its force and poured harmlessly over the cliff.

'Phew, that was close,' Peter gasped. 'Thanks, Arca. You were just in time.'

'I was in Elmesh's time. That is always sufficient,' the eagle replied.

Peter was reunited with his companions to great whoops of joy. He marvelled how Arca had not hurt him when those fearsome talons had gripped him.

'Fantastic!' cried Andrew. 'What a rescue.' He danced a jig and made faces at the dark mud across the river.

The others crowded around Arca, chattering nineteen to the dozen. Except for Flip-flop, that is, who didn't trust eagles and kept his distance. Arca might just be a bit peckish.

At that moment, a tall, lean figure stepped unnoticed from behind a tree. He stood watching the merriment with a smile.

'Hail, friends,' he called.

The babble ceased at the sound of his voice and all turned to see who spoke.

'It's Oswain!' cried Sarah with delight. She raced across and threw her arms around him. 'It's so wonderful to see you again,' she whispered.

'You, too, Sarah,' he replied. 'I have waited for this moment. Greetings, Peter. And you, Andrew. Flip-flop, I'll see you later!'

The boys shook hands warmly with their old friend. Then the King of the Great Forest of Alamore turned and looked at the princess. She came slowly towards him, with her eyes lowered.

'So, my sister Alena,' Oswain breathed. 'After such a long time. Come on, don't be afraid. I won't bite you! This is a day for great rejoicing. It is not every day that my sister pays me a visit.'

He held out his hands to her as she approached. The others watched to see how she would respond. She reached him and clasped his hands tight, then looked up earnestly into his face.

'I'm sorry,' she said.

20

Old Friends

Peter, Sarah and Andrew walked well ahead of Oswain and Princess Alena as they entered the beautiful paths of the Great Forest. Flip-flop led the way.

Everywhere flowers burst from the banks in dazzling displays of colour. Carpets of blue, red and yellow ran riot among the trees. Heady scents wafted in the light breeze and overhead the dappled sunlight fell through a canopy of fresh greenery. Stolid oaks and stately elms, ladylike birches and sweeping willows graced their path. Countless birds sang their welcoming praises in the warm summer air.

'Oh, this is so gorgeous,' exclaimed Sarah. 'Far better even than when we were here last.'

'Quite a bit different from when we first arrived. D'you remember how dead it all was?' said Peter.

'Yes, and then we got caught and thought the animals were the enemy,' Andrew reminded them. 'We couldn't have been more wrong,' he laughed.

'Still, that's all changed for ever,' said Peter. 'Oswain's seen to that.'

'What do you think will happen now that we're here?' Andrew wanted to know.

'Oh, I expect Oswain will take Alena back home and we'll go back to ours,' Peter answered.

'What about Gublak? D'you think he's dead?'

'Maybe,' Peter replied with a vague wave of his hand. He was not quite sure what had happened in the Earth-Trog's lair.

'I don't know,' said Sarah. 'I've got this funny feeling that it's not all over yet.'

'It's certainly not all over for me,' Flip-flop declared. 'Don't forget I still have to meet Oswain, and Trotter.' He looked glum. 'I'm in trouble.'

'Oh, don't worry,' said Andrew. 'We'll put a good word in for you – even though you were a bit of a twit! After all, you did get us here in the end.'

So their carefree chatter continued as they wound through the forest paths. Soon they drew near the dwellings of the forest-folk. To the children's delight everybody came out to meet them and before long they were surrounded by a hustling, chattering crowd of foxes, stoats, weasels, rabbits, badgers, squirrels, hedge-hogs and just about every other woodland creature imaginable. By the time they reached the centre of the village it was almost impossible to move for the crush.

Many of the animals remembered Peter, Sarah and Andrew and shouted their greetings. The young ones who had been born in the last year were simply curious to see these strange creatures of whom their parents spoke in such glowing terms.

'This is just amazing,' Peter laughed. 'What a sight!'

Suddenly, the hubbub dropped and, with much 'shushing', the crowd drew back so that a way opened before the children. Everyone watched as Lord Trotter came to meet them.

'Trotter!' cried Peter. The badger stopped and his bewhiskered face broke into a smile.

'My, oh my,' he cried as the children ran to join him. 'I wondered whether I would ever meet you again, my dear friends. What a delightful surprise it was when I heard that you were in Caris Meriac once more. Elmesh be praised that I have lived to see it.'

'It's absolutely wonderful to see you again, Trotter,' Sarah enthused.

'Well, my dears,' the badger went on. 'You find me a little older and a little wiser but none the worse for wear. Or Mrs Trotter for that matter.'

'You look marvellous, Trotter,' said Sarah. 'And we're so looking forward to meeting Mrs Trotter again.'

'Well, you must come at once. I hardly need tell you that she has prepared a welcome tea for you.'

'Oh, good,' said Andrew. 'So long as it's not carrot cake. I think I've seen enough of carrots for the time being!'

'What about Oswain and Alena?' Peter asked.

'They will join us soon, I expect. I imagine they wish to be alone for the moment.'

The party made its way to Trotter's delightful old cottage. Nothing much seemed to have changed, except that the grounds were well tended nowadays.

'This place is so full of memories,' Sarah sighed as they crossed the oak-beamed porch.

'Come on now, in here,' said the badger. He led them into the front room.

'Why, m'dears, how lovely to see you again,' cried Mrs Trotter. 'I've had the kettle on ever since I knew you were coming, and there's fresh bread and cakes. We've so much to talk about.'

The children greeted her with warm hugs and soon

they were busily chatting together about old times. They became so engrossed in conversation that they didn't even hear Oswain and Princess Alena come in.

'I see you have renewed your acquaintance,' he laughed. 'A good day, eh, Trotter?'

The old badger nodded and mumbled something appropriate through a mouthful of biscuit.

Oswain and the princess sat down. Sarah was glad to see she was smiling.

'Now,' said the King, 'you must tell us all that has happened to you. Some matters I have seen from afar and some I have gleaned from Alena during our walk, but I would like to hear your tale from the beginning.'

Peter began and, with the help of Sarah and Andrew, told of how they had once again entered The Land Beyond the Far Places, and of their capture by the pirates and Gublak. Andrew explained with great enthusiasm how they had escaped and then found themselves in the grip of the treacherous Dringol.

'I think you may find that he is a reformed character when you meet him again – his brother, too – but more of that later. Tell me about this Ice Maiden that Alena has spoken of in such glowing terms.'

'She's . . . well, just amazing,' said Peter.

'Brilliant,' said Andrew, and together he and his brother and sister told Oswain all they could.

Sarah noticed Oswain's keen interest. 'Hey, Peter, have you still got that crystal?' she asked.

He dug into his pocket. 'Yes, here it is.'

'Well, I think Oswain should have it,' she said firmly.

Peter had no objections and handed it over.

Oswain gazed in wonder at the jewel.

'This is surely a stone of destiny,' he murmured. 'I must seek out this Ice Maiden. I am sure it was she who helped me too.'

'Why don't you have the stone set in a ring?' Sarah suggested.

He looked her straight in the eyes but her face was a picture of smiling innocence.

'Maybe I shall,' he said turning the jewel in his fingers. 'Maybe I shall.'

'Arca's rescue was brilliant,' said Peter. 'Was he here all the time – you know, waiting for the right moment?'

'No, not at all, and nor was I.' Oswain explained all that had happened to him. 'Once we had put matters to rights with the Dweorgs we set off at a cracking pace to catch up with you, for at that time we all thought that the wolves were after you. We reached the hollow – an evil place that – and soon realised that there were many other feet, so we guessed that Gublak had been there and we feared that you were already in his grip. It was then that Arca appeared. I was so relieved, for he could bear me far faster than my legs could carry me. Yet instead of taking me to Gublak he brought me straight to the Great Forest. He obviously knew of your true whereabouts.'

'Stiggle and I had gone to the Enchanted Glade to seek the wisdom of Elmesh,' Trotter explained. 'It seems our prayers have been answered with Arca's arrival.'

So the tales continued and the shadows began to lengthen in the golden glow of sunset. Peter looked out of the leaded window.

'Can we visit Aldred's memorial?' he asked.

'By all means,' Oswain smiled. 'Then on to the

Enchanted Glade, eh?'

'Oh, yes please,' they chorused.

'I will stay here if you don't mind,' said Trotter. 'But do return to us and stay the night, won't you? Beds have been prepared for everyone.'

They thanked Mr and Mrs Trotter for their hospitality and then made their way to Aldred's memorial. There, before the statue of the heroic stoat who in their previous adventure had given his life to save Peter, Sarah and Andrew, they stood in solemn silence.

Finally Oswain ushered the children away and led them in the direction of the Enchanted Glade.

On the way there, Sarah had a word with Alena. 'I don't know why, but I feel I should give you this,' she said, and from her jerkin she gave the last of the turtle dove's tail feathers to the princess. The princess tucked it into the waistband of her trousers but said nothing.

A tingling sense of expectancy filled them as they approached the sentinel stones that marked the entrance to the glade. The air buzzed with life and when they passed the stones a golden glory momentarily blinded their eyes as the last rays of the setting sun blazed a trail across the glen.

The first stars of evening came peeking out from the blue canopy above as the five approached Elmere, the Star-Pool, alongside which rested the famed Merestone. Each one felt the awesome power of the place and their voices were hushed.

'It's so special,' Sarah said. 'There's nowhere else like it in all the world.' She wanted to say more, but there were no words to express what was in her heart.

'Often I come here to learn the ways of Elmesh,' said

Oswain. 'You speak truly, Sarah. It is a place of wonder.'

Each of the three children took their turn to look into the enchanted pool but, slightly to their disappointment, they saw only their own faces.

'It is not for you to see visions this time,' Oswain said. 'But, Alena, you may see much this night by the light of Elrilion.'

The princess did not reply. She was overwhelmed by the enchantment of the place and gazed in wonder at the pearl-like drops of water that fell into the glowing pool.

Sarah was wistful. 'I wish we could stay the night here,' she said. 'I could live for ever in this place.'

Oswain smiled. 'I am sure you could, Sarah, but you must not neglect the hospitality of Lord and Lady Trotter.' He glanced at the evening sky. 'Soon it will be dark and Elrilion will have risen. You must return to their cottage.'

'Aren't you coming with us?' Andrew asked.

Oswain shook his head. 'Not yet. Nor Alena. For we must speak alone of many things and see what we shall see in this place. Mind your steps now, but you will find the way with ease.'

The three children reluctantly did as they were told and left the enchanted glade.

'D'you think Oswain's going to tell Alena off?' asked Andrew.

'I doubt it somehow,' his brother replied. 'I expect he'll make her completely well and sort everything out. That's why she was meant to come here, I reckon.'

'Oh well, that's about it for us, I suppose,' Sarah sighed. 'We've done what we were sent for. But I can't help feeling that there's . . .'

She never finished her sentence. A rough hand clamped over her mouth and she was pulled to the ground by two dark figures.

Before Peter and Andrew could do anything to help, other shadowy shapes darted from the undergrowth and leapt upon them, also. They scuffled and struggled with all their might but without success. Andrew tried to wriggle free but he was no match for his assailants and was soon held captive. Peter put up a good fight and almost managed to pull Sarah free, but a blow to the back of his head sent him reeling into unconsciousness.

'Well done, me hearties,' hissed a voice. 'Tie 'em up and let's be out of 'ere. Reckon Cap'n Gaspar and 'is Eminence'll be 'ighly pleased with tonight's little catch.'

21

The Past Revealed

'See, Elrilion has risen,' said Oswain. He directed Princess Alena's attention to the bright star that hung low in the sky yet greatly outshone its companions. The Enchanted Glade seemed to become even more alive beneath its brilliance, and the pearl-like drops of water that fed the Star-Pool from the rock above gleamed in response.

Oswain spoke solemnly to his adopted sister. 'The time has come for you to know the truth about yourself, Alena. You are a child of destiny, as I am myself. I gazed into this same pool and discovered my fate. It was not easy for me and it may not be so for you.'

The princess returned his look. 'I don't think I am afraid,' she said. 'But would you hold my hand, please?'

He smiled and took it in his own. Together they approached the enchanted pool. Princess Alena felt a mixture of curiosity and awe as she leaned over the water and looked in.

At first she saw only her own reflection. Then the waters swirled and pictures began to form. A landscape unfolded before her and she heard a rushing noise as her eye raced over fields and rivers, across plains and mountains, until it came to rest on a stern northern land of craggy peaks and broad lakes. Imposing castles, mighty fortresses and vast cities arrayed themselves before her. This was a rich and proud kingdom.

In a moment, the vision changed and she saw a strong, tall man clothed in diamond-studded black leather and seated upon a magnificent throne. His features were as proud and stern as the land over which he ruled. The princess could feel the power of his personality reach right into her. Something stirred in her heart and she wondered at the greatness of this man to whom surely mighty empires bowed down.

A fair young woman, heavily pregnant, stood beside him. She was soon to give birth.

'It is Surin of Traun,' whispered Oswain. 'He is the most powerful dark lord of the northern realms.'

The scene changed and they saw that a girl child had been born. Now the mighty ruler stood in a dimly lit room, holding the baby before his gods. A black crow was perched upon his shoulder. Princess Alena heard the words within her mind: 'To the dark powers of Kraan I dedicate this child and call her Astar. By my oath, a mighty queen shall she be, as invincible as I myself. The lands of the West, and all Alamore, shall be her domain. They will serve your power and bow before my rule.'

The princess looked in wonder. She caught a glimpse of the child's mother peering around the door with anguish written on her face.

The waters swirled once more and she could see the fair mother fleeing for her life with her baby clutched tightly to her. Fear and dread filled her face. The journey seemed unending until at last it brought her to a city that Princess Alena recognised as Elmar. Still the woman fled, twisting and turning among the narrow streets and always glancing behind her, until at length she came within sight of the palace gates.

Yet, even as she made to enter, two strangely robed figures emerged from the shadows, one tall and lean, the other short and round.

A knife flashed from the hand of the taller one and Princess Alena gasped as she watched it plunge between the shoulder blades of the fugitive woman. She cried out and fell dead. One of the assailants rushed to seize the child but before he could do so, the palace guards came running and the two figures withdrew again into the shadows.

The baby girl was still alive and Princess Alena stared transfixed as she saw her borne into the palace.

In a final vision, the King and Queen of Elmar appeared, standing before the Lord Chancellor with the baby held in the Queen's arms. The princess heard the adoption order read and saw the Star Stone placed around the child's neck. A crow perched nearby. There could be no doubt that the child born to Surin was none other than Princess Alena herself.

The scene faded until she could see only her own face in the water. Strange emotions filled her heart. At last she knew who she was. Her name was Astar. She thought of the proud warrior king in all his splendour – her father – the man Oswain called Surin. She felt the awesome power of his oath to the dark gods.

Then the treachery of her mother's death angered her. Yet why had she fled to the western capital in the first place? Perhaps the gods had dictated her steps. Would they have their way no matter what? Was the princess meant to serve their ends? Then what of the Star Stone?

Was it to help her or was it a barrier to her true destiny?

Oswain released her hand and drew back. His face was grim.

'Then you are Astar, the offspring of Surin.' He spoke gravely. 'He is the sworn enemy of our kingdoms. By rights I should have you slain or at least banished, yet here you stand as my sister. What a strange fortune this is.'

The princess was trembling and on the verge of tears. 'I don't understand all this,' she said. 'If only I had not looked into the pool!'

'The revelations of the Star-Pool are not always a comfort, but nonetheless they serve great purposes,' Oswain answered. He shook his head. 'I pity you, princess, for the choice that lies before you.'

She appeared perplexed, so he explained. 'For many years the house of Surin of Traun has plagued the western lands. The king, your real father, is a great man; he is ambitious and ruthless. His empire is mighty, but he is not satisfied. Nor are the gods of Kraan whom he serves. Their evil influence reached through him into my own country years ago and corrupted even the one I loved. I am no friend of Surin!'

Princess Alena had grown pale.

'Since then,' he continued, 'our strength has increased and we dwell secure. Surin cannot break the power of Elmesh that guards our borders. Yet times may change. The rule of my father has been long and wise, but, alas, he ages and must go the way of all mortal creatures.'

'And Surin, my real father, knows this?' Princess Alena asked.

'Indeed,' replied Oswain.

'Then won't you reign in his place, since you are the eldest?'

'My family has chosen to reign only in accord with Elmesh's will. Thus, I was destined to rule the eastern lands of the Great Forest of Alamore. Yet who will fill the throne of Elmar when my father passes?' He gave the princess a penetrating look. 'It was to be you, Alena. Indeed, I see now that it shall be you. But as friend or foe? That is the question.'

Princess Alena looked aghast at her brother. The truth had dawned. She was indeed a daughter of destiny. Even now the conflict arose in her heart. Should she serve her father, Surin, in accordance with his oath? Or should she choose the way of her adoptive parents and reign in alliance with Oswain? Whatever her choice, one or other of them would become her mortal enemy.

'I don't know how to answer that question,' she sighed. 'What will become of me? And where does Gublak fit into all this?'

Oswain looked sadly at the girl. 'I believe I can now answer your last question. As Trotter gazed into the Star-Pool, seeking to bring us aid from afar, he learned that someone had plied Gublak with many favours and at last bewitched him so that he would covet the Star Stone more than anything else in the world.

'He did not know then who it was, but I know now that it is Surin, your father, who is behind all this. He has waited all these years until you should come of age. Now he seeks to make his move. Crow was his avenue to you and it was he who planted the seeds of rebellion that made you run away from home. Gublak did the rest.'

'But why does everyone want to take the Star Stone

from me?' Princess Alena wailed. 'I don't even know why I have it. Gublak said it was worthless to me and . . .'

'He was lying,' Oswain interrupted. 'Greed always uses deceit, and he tried to fool you into thinking the jewel was unimportant.'

'But he wanted to use it himself,' said the princess. 'Would it have worked?'

Oswain shook his head. 'No, the Star Stone will serve only the will of Elmesh. It would be useless to Gublak. However, the bewitchment does not let him know that. So he desires it still. Your father wanted him to take it from you because then you would no longer be protected from him and the powers he serves.'

Princess Alena was silent. She thought again about her real father. He was a magnificent warrior king and she knew his blood ran in her veins. Visions of grandeur passed before her. She saw herself standing with him and imagined his pride in her, Queen Astar, ruler of the West. Gublak had lied; she was of royal blood. Only the Star Stone kept her from living as the daughter of Surin.

Then she thought of her adoptive parents. Deep down she loved them and she could see how they had pitied her and shown great kindness. She looked into the strong face of Oswain and felt the wealth of goodness that flowed from him and all his domain. She could see now that it was her father's blood that had made her wary of him.

Oswain spoke again. 'My parents gave you the Star Stone not just to protect you from danger,' he said. 'They did not even know who your parents were. They bestowed it upon you to make you truly one of the royal family, Alena. They had no other children besides me so they looked upon you as a gift from Elmesh and chose you as heir to the throne. The jewel gives you the right and power to reign with Elmesh's blessing. Do you see its importance? It is the very key to the throne.'

She nodded but said nothing.

'You are now thirteen years of age,' Oswain continued. 'For you, it is the age of decision. You must choose freely whether to accept the Star Stone and serve Elmesh or to relinquish it and serve your father, Surin. It will be no easy decision, for many destinies turn upon it and much conflict will follow.'

'I must think,' the princess replied. 'But not in this place. For here I could easily choose to serve Elmesh but I cannot say it would be so when I left.'

Oswain nodded. 'Then let us depart and return to Lord and Lady Trotter's house. There you may consider your decision in private.'

*   *   *

It didn't take them long to reach the badgers' cottage and they were silent all the way.

Upon their arrival they were surprised to see lights in the window.

'Thank Elmesh you have returned,' exclaimed Trotter as they entered. 'I could not sleep and I feared some misadventure had befallen you.'

'No, we are quite safe,' Oswain smiled. 'But thank you for your concern, my friend. Are the children safely tucked up?'

'Are they not with you?' gasped the badger.

Oswain shook his head. Trotter staggered to an armchair. He sat down weakly.

'Oh dear,' he gasped. 'Then something has gone terribly amiss. I knew it. We haven't seen them since they left with you.'

Oswain looked grim. He glanced sharply at Princess Alena. 'I suspect the work of Gublak. It seems his evil has penetrated even the sacred reaches of the Great Forest.'

He turned to the badger. 'Trotter, we must rouse the forest-folk. I'll do that while you get Stiggle. You come with me, Alena. I do not want you out of my sight!'

They rushed from the cottage and hurried to the village dwellings. It didn't take long to gather a large crowd of animals, although there was much yawning and murmuring. Oswain swiftly explained what had happened and the muttering ceased.

'Find out what you can and return here,' he urged. 'And quickly. We have no time to lose.'

At once, the loyal animals sped in all directions to search for tracks.

It didn't prove difficult to find where the scuffle had occurred, and the information was swiftly relayed to Oswain by a hare named Fleetfoot.

Minutes later he was joined by Stiggle and Fumble and Mumble.

Oswain filled them in on the night's events. 'Stiggle, you and I will go with Fleetfoot to see what has been found. Fumble and Mumble, you are to stay here with the princess. Do not let her out of your sight and especially do not let her remove the jewel she wears about her neck. Is that understood?'

'The matter is perfectly clear, sir,' answered Mumble with unaccustomed clarity.

'It will be our pleasure,' smiled Fumble and he saluted smartly.

A cluster of animals met Oswain and Stiggle when they arrived at the scene with Fleetfoot. He pointed a way through the damaged undergrowth.

'That's where they dragged them,' said Stiggle. 'We must follow their trail. But keep your eyes open, everyone. The enemy may still be about.'

The animals followed the scent with great stealth, keeping their eyes open for trouble, but soon the excitement of the chase caught some of the younger ones and they hared ahead. However, they were brought to an abrupt halt at the ford in the river and had to wait for the others. A lot of muddy footprints showed that this was where the brigands had crossed.

'Do we carry on, sir?' puffed Stiggle as he and Oswain reached the ford.

'Yes, but with greater care,' Oswain replied. He glanced at the sky. 'It is not long until dawn and there is little cover over the river. Tell some of the animals to return and fetch weapons. I have a feeling we shall need them before the day is very old.'

Half the group sped off to follow Stiggle's orders while the rest accompanied Oswain. They were soon within range of the enemy camp. The glow of a fire gave it away and Oswain motioned everyone to stop.

'We must wait for weapons,' he whispered to Stiggle. 'The goblin will have wolves prowling the camp. It's no use attacking like this. Let's just hope the children are still all right.'

The weasel agreed. 'Then let's leave the trail and make our way around to the higher ground on the right. That'll enable us to give a bit of surprise. Our folk will find us easily enough when they return with the arms.'

* * *

Back in the village the two mice sat on the ground with the princess. She looked glum. Fumble and Mumble exchanged glances.

'Perhaps you should recite some poetry, Mumble,' suggested Fumble.

'Well, youmiaswelldo cartwheelsthen,' he replied.

'Personally I would rather be asleep,' Fumble answered. 'I'm absolutely exhausted.'

Mumble addressed the princess. 'Er, um, wot-shorname, please?'

'It is Alena,' she answered shortly. 'But you should call me "Your Royal Highness".'

'Oh, um, yes, yeroliness,' he mumbled, a bit put off.

That put paid to conversation for a good long while until suddenly the princess leapt to her feet. The mice jerked in surprise and Fumble fell over as he tried to get up too quickly.

'I don't feel I like the idea of being kept a prisoner, particularly by mice,' she declared haughtily. 'I shall take a walk.'

'I'm sorry, er, your royal highness,' said Mumble,

speaking very clearly, 'but we've got our orders and we're to stay here with you.'

'I should look over there first, if I were you,' said the princess and she pointed with her finger to something behind them. The two mice turned and fell for the oldest trick in the book. In a flash the princess was off.

'Quick, she's making a bolt for it,' cried Fumble. 'After her!'

Whether it was his fault or not, the two mice somehow collided in the confusion and fell into a confused heap on the ground. By the time they had untangled themselves, the princess was nowhere to be seen.

'Now we really are in trouble,' Fumble groaned.

22
Alena Chooses

In the grey dawn Oswain surveyed the scene from the low, bushy hill where he and his party crouched on the north side of Gublak's camp. They were nearer than he had first thought, and he could plainly make out the prowling wolves, as well as pirates and Urgils. However, what immediately caught his attention were three stakes to which were tied three figures. He guessed at once they were Peter, Sarah and Andrew. Stiggle moved up alongside him to take a look.

Before the weasel could comment they heard a disturbance behind them. Fearing the worst, they retreated in haste to rejoin their companions, only to be greeted by the sight of a distressed mouse, desperately trying to catch his breath and stumbling towards them.

'What is it?' Oswain demanded. 'What has happened?'

'The princess has escaped. I'm sorry, sir,' gasped Fumble.

Oswain shook his head and groaned.

'Where's Mumble?' Stiggle demanded. 'I suppose he's tied himself up with his own tongue!'

'No, he hasn't,' Fumble replied in defence of his friend. 'He's gone after the princess. I've run straight here.'

Ignoring the question as to whether Fumble could run

straight anywhere, Stiggle asked what direction he thought the princess had taken.

'I left Mumble to follow her trail after we crossed the ford,' said Fumble.

'Then she's making for the enemy camp, I reckon,' Stiggle said.

Oswain agreed and dashed back through the bushes to his vantage point. From there he could make out the slim figure of Princess Alena running straight towards Gublak's camp.

'We've got to stop her somehow,' hissed Stiggle as he joined him.

'Yes,' said Oswain and made to rise. But something seemed to check him. 'No, she must choose for herself. I must not force her. Let the princess face the goblin alone and decide her own fate!' He spoke grimly and Stiggle wondered at the seriousness of his tone.

* * *

Peter, Sarah and Andrew had fared badly since their capture by the pirates. They had been bound and gagged, then humped roughly through the forest, across the ford and on into Gublak's presence.

The goblin was delighted with the catch and immediately ordered the children to be tied to the stakes.

His green eyes flashed in the firelight as he addressed them. He spoke smoothly. 'I would have preferred the princess herself. But no matter. You will be useful in the bargaining. The Star Stone in exchange for your lives, eh? I do not think there will be much resistance.'

The children were quite helpless and entirely at the mercy of the goblin. Despair engulfed them as he left them for his tent. A prowling wolf brushed against Sarah's leg and she gave a muffled scream from behind her gag. Andrew stared blankly at the pirates and the Urgils gathered around the fire. It would be a long night.

For Peter especially the hours dragged by with agonising slowness. From the moment he regained consciousness his head had not ceased to throb. He would have done anything just to have been able to rub the bruise. All night long he battled with the sickening pain and a despondency that almost overwhelmed him. He dare not lose heart. Help must come from somewhere.

Dawn brought little relief from the discomfort but it made him feel a little better. Oswain would find a way to rescue them, he felt sure. After all, this was not the first time they had been in a tight spot.

He was just regaining confidence when, to his dismay, he saw Princess Alena running alone towards the camp. She could not know she was heading for trouble, he thought. He tried to warn her, but the gag stopped him producing anything more than a muffled grunt.

The princess slowed to a walk, then to his amazement strode boldly right into the centre of the encampment. Her arrival caused quite a commotion and the goblin himself emerged from his tent to see what all the fuss was about. An oily smile lit up his fat face when he saw who it was.

'Ah, Princess, so you have come to me at last. You will see that your friends have already joined us.' He glanced towards the children. 'It has been a long time since we last spoke and I have eagerly awaited this moment.' His voice took on a steely edge. 'I need hardly tell an intelligent girl such as yourself what my terms are.'

Peter stared wide-eyed at the princess. He willed her to flee even though it didn't look as if she had a chance. If only he could do something. She glanced coldly in the direction of the bound children, then back to Gublak.

Only then did it dawn on Peter that Princess Alena may have chosen, after all, to flee the forest and join forces with Gublak. Oswain would never have sent her unprotected like this. Peter's heart sank. All the effort that they had made to bring the princess to a place of safety had been wasted.

Just then, he felt an odd movement behind him. Someone was tugging at his bonds. Peter jumped with surprise and tried to twist his head to see who it was.

'Keep still,' hissed a voice. 'Is me, Mumble. Pretendnothinsappnin anlookstraitahed.'

Peter could have shouted for joy and really had to fight hard not to give the game away. Mumble seemed to take ages gnawing at the knots, but actually it was only a matter of moments before the intrepid mouse succeeded. To Peter's intense relief, his bonds fell away.

* * *

Tired and weary, Grumble smiled and twitched his whiskers at the sight of the River Wendle. He had travelled slowly and rested often but now another hour should see him home. Dawn was breaking so he stopped to rummage around for some berries and seeds. No sense in rushing the last part of the journey, he decided.

Ten minutes later he was ready for the trail – and it was then that he received the shock of his life. Standing before him were two Dweorgs, and one of them he recognised at once. It was Brankleshanks. Grumble groaned in despair and raised his paws in surrender. If only he hadn't stopped for breakfast.

Yet, to his amazement, Brankleshanks, instead of drawing his bow and shooting him, came over and knelt down before him.

'Do not be afraid,' he said. 'We are well met and I am relieved for your safety. To you I owe the deepest apologies that my heart can offer. I treated you cruelly for my own greed. It was wrong of me and I beg your forgiveness.'

Grumble could scarcely believe his ears and he remained for some moments with his front paws raised in the air before he realised that this was now unnecessary.

Then Dringol introduced himself and explained what had happened on the mountain. 'We are Dweorgs of the Oath, so we are pledged to serve Oswain and all those with him.'

'Well, I am mightily glad to hear it,' said Grumble. 'Apologies accepted, of course. But where is Oswain now?'

'Ah, that's the other matter,' Dringol answered. 'We were racing after Gublak and his thugs in the hope of catching them and rescuing the princess when out of the blue we heard a wild screech. I tell you, it sent shivers down my spine.'

'Then a great white eagle plummeted out of the sky,' Brankleshanks continued. 'We thought it was going to attack us but it landed and seemed to know Oswain.'

'Arca!' breathed Grumble. 'Then all is well.'

'The eagle carried Oswain off, though in a direction we would not have expected. Oswain told us that we were free to do as we wished,' said Dringol.

'So, you decided to come to Alamore?'

'We hoped to assist Oswain but as yet we have found no sign of a battle.'

'Then we must press on to the Great Forest,' said Grumble. 'We may still be needed.'

So, the three set off in haste, but Brankleshanks insisted that he carry Grumble, both for speed and in token of his apology.

* * *

Princess Alena's mind had been in a whirl since she had looked into the Star-Pool. The knowledge of who she really was and the awful choice that lay before her had left her completely dazed. A thousand conflicting thoughts battled away in her head and she really did not know what to do next.

It was the discovery of the children's capture that had helped her make up her mind. It meant Gublak was nearby, presumably just across the river. She had determined then to escape and get to him. For Princess Alena knew with terrible certainty that the only way she could make her decision was to come face to face with the goblin himself.

Evading the two mice had proved all too easy. She fled in the general direction of the river, prepared to swim across if necessary, but found the ford and was soon on the other bank. From the footprints and broken twigs lying around, it had not been difficult for her to find the way to the goblin's camp from there on.

The sun was just beginning to light the sky behind her as she entered Gublak's camp.

'Give me the Star Stone,' the goblin now demanded. 'Let me have it and your friends go free. You may join me or go your own way, as you wish. But the Star Stone must be mine.'

His eyes glittered with greed and he watched as she slowly drew out the jewel from inside her blouse so that it hung in view about her neck on its silver chain.

'Ah, how beautiful it is,' he sighed. 'No use to you, of course. But beautiful to me. Any reward you ask shall be yours, Princess. Only let me possess it.'

At this point Princess Alena felt nothing but loathing for the goblin's greed and was about to refuse him, when a very strange thing began to happen.

As she looked at Gublak, his whole appearance started to change and in place of his fat green figure she saw instead the tall, stern form of Surin. She gasped with shock. Her head reeled. Gublak was not Surin, was he? Surely not!

Yet it was without doubt Surin's steely eyes that seemed to bore right through her. She tried to move, but her legs would not obey. She was spellbound.

'Take off the Star Stone,' a voice ordered. 'Give it to the goblin. You are my child. Astar is your name, and as the daughter of Surin shall you be known.' The figure's lips curled into a smile. 'The gods of Kraan have directed your destiny well. Now the time has come for you to rule, my child. Long enough have you been slave to the contemptible ways of the Western kingdom. Remove this chain, cast off this trash, and all will bow to serve your will.'

'Yes, Father,' the princess answered meekly. 'I will do as you say.'

All eyes were upon her as she reached behind her neck for the clasp.

None of those who viewed the transformation or who heard the strange voice from Gublak's lips understood what it all meant, least of all the three children. But Peter realised that some sort of enchantment had taken place. He also knew that there was only one chance left. Without any further thought, he took it. He sprinted as fast as he could and hurled himself at the goblin's legs (for it was, of course, Gublak after all) and brought him crashing to the ground with a rugby tackle worthy of the first team.

So unexpected was his action that it was over before anyone could stop him. The goblin howled with rage at the assault.

In an instant, Peter was surrounded.

Ulris stood panting over him, his breath foul and his jaws slavering. The wolf glanced at his master who was struggling to his feet. He awaited the order to tear out Peter's throat. Gublak was breathing heavily as he rose.

His eyes were hard with rage but he held out a restraining hand in the wolf's direction. The bewitched goblin was quite unaware that Surin had spoken through him. He assumed Princess Alena was simply giving in to his demands.

'One moment, Ulris,' he grated. 'Your foolish friend tries my patience, Princess. He thinks he can prevent what must surely come to pass. He has failed, of course. Now, the Star Stone, if you please.'

Princess Alena was as amazed as anyone at Peter's sudden attack. On the surface it seemed such a hopeless gesture. Yet it had not been in vain. The vision of Surin had passed and the spell was broken. At that moment, some powerful feeling stirred within her, the like of which she had never felt before. She faced Gublak square on.

'No! The jewel shall not be yours.' Her voice rang out across the dell and her eyes shone with a new light. 'Hear this, all you powers,' she proclaimed. 'Astar I shall never be. Surin I renounce. I, Alena, accept the Star Stone. I shall serve Elmesh!'

An angry rumble of thunder sounded far away in the north, though only the keenest ears could hear it.

At once, an amazing transformation took place before everyone's astonished gaze. The princess seemed to be lost in a bright blue light and the air was filled with a strange music. As the light slowly faded, gone were her tattered travelling clothes and she wore instead a shimmering silver-blue gown. A tiara adorned her golden hair.

Gublak and his evil band looked on in horror. Peter had tears in his eyes as he gazed up at her from where he lay on the ground. Sarah and Andrew would have cheered if their gags had let them.

Then the sun broke above the horizon and in its morning glory the princess seemed basked in a halo of gold. The wolves, the pirates and the Urgils drew back in dread, leaving Gublak alone to face her. Only Ulris dared to stand firm. Peter lay on the ground to his side.

Oswain had seen and heard all this from where he lay hidden and now he stood up. His strong voice resounded from the hill. 'Hail, my sister Alena!' He waved and started towards her.

Princess Alena gazed at him with a dazzling smile. 'Hail, my brother Oswain!' she cried in response and raised her hand, holding out the feather of a turtle dove that shone with burnished silver. The air seemed to crackle with life as though some immense energy had been released into the atmosphere. Everyone's hair stood on end. Then, to the amazement of all, a beam of silver fire flared from hand to hand between Oswain and his radiant sister. Awesome in their united strength, the two turned their faces towards Gublak.

23

Fight to the Finish

Everything seemed to happen at once. The beam of light joining Oswain and Princess Alena vanished as suddenly as it had appeared and in its place each found themselves grasping a glittering silver sword. Oswain reacted immediately. With a triumphant shout he held the weapon aloft and led the forest-folk in a wild charge down the hillside.

Gublak took one look at the assault. 'Attack them!' he screamed. 'Don't let them get the princess. I want her taken alive.'

He rushed forward to seize Alena. Peter, seeing what was happening, reacted at once and lashed out with his feet from where he lay. The goblin stumbled and cursed. His face twisted with hatred.

'Ulris, kill him,' he commanded.

The leader of the wolf pack needed no second bidding. He leapt towards Peter, his wild yellow eyes blazing and his terrible fangs glinting in the sun as he pounced for the kill.

'Look out, Peter,' Princess Alena cried.

With a desperate twist of his body Peter threw himself to one side. The wolf's claws missed by millimetres and Peter felt the brush of fur against his face.

Princess Alena sprang forward and faced the snarling wolf as Peter scrambled to his feet. Ulris's hackles rose, his eyes grew slanty and every muscle tensed within his lean frame. The princess flicked a glance at the gleaming sword. It tingled in her grasp. Her heart thumped wildly. She knew one of them would have to die.

They circled one another warily, both looking for the moment to attack. The wolf seemed to grow larger and more powerful in Princess Alena's eyes. Some terrible spirit glowered from within him and for a second her heart quailed. Ulris sensed it and seized his opportunity. Uttering a soul destroying howl, he hurled himself at the princess's throat.

'No,' screeched Gublak. 'I must have her alive.'

He was too late. The wolf had leapt to kill.

A huge shadow seemed to envelop the princess as she felt the full unearthly force of the wild wolf-spirit. She fell backwards and in one final, desperate gesture she thrust upwards with her sword. Then that blade, surely forged by Elmesh himself, and burning with a fiery light, plunged into the heart of the wolf.

Ulris gave one last howl, twisted away and fell, to rise no more.

Princess Alena lay panting on the ground. She looked at the sword then at the dead wolf. A tremor ran through her body as she thought of what might have happened. She wanted to cry.

But there was no time for that. Peter was by her side helping her to her feet. Oswain and his troops were upon their foes and already a fierce battle was raging all around them. At once the princess found herself in conflict with an Urgil, but his blade was no match for hers and he fell, mortally wounded. Peter seized the dropped sword and began to fight alongside her. Together, they tried to hew their way through the enemy to where they could see Oswain's sword flashing in the sun.

Meanwhile, Mumble had not been idle; he had released both Sarah and Andrew – but being unarmed the three of them stood in great danger.

'Peter! Alena! Help!' yelled Sarah above the din of battle.

They turned at the sound of her voice and immediately began to fight their way across to their companions' defence.

Yet they need not have worried for at that very moment two Dweorgs armed with fearsome battle axes and crossbows leapt to their aid, while a brave and defiant mouse with a scarred ear cheered them on.

The heat of the battle rose; swords crashed and the cries of the warriors filled the air. Wolves hurled themselves into the fray, intent on avenging their leader's death. Urgils thrashed their reptilian tails in deadly sweeps. Their combined forces outnumbered the brave forest-folk almost two to one but, urged on by Oswain, the woodland creatures stoutly stood their ground.

Stiggle wove in and out among the foe. His sword thrusts were deadly and many an Urgil regretted having confronted the fearless weasel.

A cry for help caught his attention. Fumble was in trouble. Somehow he had fallen and three Urgils surrounded him, intent on his death. Stiggle leapt to his comrade's aid. His sword sliced through the air and one of the Urgils fell.

'That evens things up a bit,' he cried. 'Come on, Fumble. On your feet.'

The mouse leapt up and together they engaged the

two remaining Urgils. It didn't take long to defeat them.

'Thanks,' puffed Fumble. 'I thought I was done for just then.'

'All in a day's work,' Stiggle laughed. 'Hey, there's Oswain. Look at that sword. Did you ever see anything like it?'

They watched for a moment. Oswain's gleaming blade seemed scarcely to touch his adversaries before they fell. It looked as if nothing could stop him.

'There's a wolf after Fleetfoot,' exclaimed Grumble. 'We'd better help. He's only got a club.'

They dashed to his assistance, but a deadly bolt from the bow of Dringol put paid to the wolf before they could reach him.

Gublak stood heavily defended by his guards, from where he continually shrieked orders to his troops. He suddenly noticed that up to now the pirates had held back from the fighting.

'Come, you cowards,' cried the goblin. 'A thousand pieces of gold to whoever kills that man.' He pointed to the figure of Oswain. 'And two thousand gold pieces to whoever takes the princess alive.'

That did it. 'Come on, me hearties,' cried Captain Gaspar. 'Let's kill these landlubbers. Slit their throats!'

The band of brigands drew their knives and, full of menace, advanced into the fray.

Yet hardly had they started fighting when something happened that changed their minds completely. An awesome, bloodcurdling screech rent the air and they saw the mighty Arca sweep into the conflict. Huge white wings thrashed as Elmesh's servant created havoc among his enemies. His eye was on the wolves and his fierce talons plunged into one after another, bringing instant death.

The band of pirates halted in their tracks and dismay filled their hearts as they saw this terrifying addition to the enemy.

'Come on, lads, let's get out of 'ere,' shouted one of the pirates. 'Never mind the gold. I want to keep me 'ead!'

'Hold yer ground,' Captain Gaspar commanded his men – but they had seen enough. The pirates turned and fled for their lives.

'Come back, you fools,' screamed Gublak, but even he could not match the terror of the great eagle.

Captain Gaspar hesitated a moment but realised all was lost. He joined his fleeing crew.

Nobody ever knew what happened to those cruel cut-throats. Rumour has it that their flight took them into the marshlands and it may be that the Earth-Trog, denied all else, claimed them as victims. Whatever the truth, they were never seen again.

The battle was turning in favour of Oswain and his companions. Those Urgils and wolves not already dead were weakening under the onslaught. Soon even the ones surrounding Gublak had endured enough and, in spite of his threats, they fled the battlefield, though many could not outrun the vengeful arrows of the two Dweorgs.

It was all over.

Stiggle found himself next to Peter. 'Just like old times,' he laughed.

Peter grinned and wiped the sweat from his brow.

'You were brilliant,' raved Andrew as he and his sister joined them.

'I really thought Ulris had got you,' said Sarah. She put her arm around her brother's waist. 'I'm glad he didn't.'

Peter smiled. 'So am I,' he said with feeling. He looked towards Princess Alena. 'Still, it's done now. They're all dead.'

'Except for Gublak,' said Andrew. 'Look, Oswain and Alena have got him.'

The four of them made their way among the slain to where Oswain and the princess stood with their captive. The goblin was sullen.

'Well done,' said Oswain. 'All of you. You have shown great courage.'

'Yes, thank you for helping me,' said Princess Alena. 'If you hadn't been here I would have lost everything. I really don't know how to thank you enough.'

The children felt a bit sheepish all of a sudden.

'It was nothing really,' Peter muttered.

'Nonsense,' Oswain declared. 'Once more you have come to our aid. Elmesh be praised for sending you.'

'Hear, hear,' piped a small voice.

'Hello, Mumble,' said Oswain. 'You too have done well. You were very brave to go into the enemy camp like that. I am proud of you, my friend.'

The mouse mumbled something in reply. The others laughed.

Just then Dringol and Brankleshanks joined the victorious group. Oswain greeted them. 'I see your oath was not in vain,' he said.

'Such an oath is unbreakable. Did we not say that we are your servants?' Brankleshanks answered.

'Are many of our folk wounded?' Oswain enquired of Stiggle.

The weasel looked around. 'Very few I think, sir. But I'll go and check.'

They turned their attention to the defeated goblin.

'Your greed has caused much evil,' Oswain said. 'And to what end? The Star Stone would have done you no good, and in any case it was destined never to be yours. You were doomed to fail and fail you have. Your one hope lies in renouncing your desire for the jewel.'

This was too much for the defeated goblin. He began to gasp and a rattling sound emerged from his throat. His bony hands clenched and unclenched as a final madness came over him. He stared at Princess Alena and his eyes bulged wildly. The Star Stone radiated its blue fire, more beautiful than ever before. It seemed to hypnotise the crazed goblin.

'No, it's not true. I have come too far. I must have it,' he screamed. 'Give it to me. Give it to me!'

Before anyone could stop him, he stumbled towards the princess and with one last desperate cry flung himself upon her. She gasped as his greedy fingers closed around the jewel. With a savage wrench he tore the Star Stone from her neck and staggered away clutching his glowing prize.

'It's all mine,' he gloated. 'The Star Stone is all mine at last!'

Everyone present was stunned by his sudden action. Princess Alena could only stare horror-struck after him. She clutched at her throat and a terrible feeling of foreboding came over her. Oswain at once made to go for the goblin but the evil creature turned on him.

'Do not touch me,' he snarled. 'You were mistaken. You, and your friends. Nobody can stop me. . . . Aaaghh!'

Gublak screamed. His face contorted and his body writhed in agony. White smoke began to pour from between his fingers. Desperately, he tried to fling the Star Stone from him, but he found he couldn't. It seemed stuck to his hand.

The smoke gave way to a brilliant blue light that dazzled the eyes of the onlookers. They heard a last long wail of despair from the goblin, then a dull thud. The light faded and there on the ground lay Gublak, with the Star Stone by his side. He was dead.

Before anyone could move, a mournful howl sounded from the north. Everyone spun round to see what it was. To their dismay, they saw racing across the Waste Plains the grey twisted funnel of a whirlwind. They were right in its path. Cold, hard evil filled the rushing air.

'Surin's work!' muttered Oswain. 'He's coming for Alena.'

He strode forward to where the Star Stone lay and touched the broken chain with the tip of his sword. There was a hiss and a bright spark. In an instant the chain was restored – but he did not pick it up. Instead, Oswain turned to face his sister.

Princess Alena seemed to be in a trance. She stared wide-eyed at the fast-approaching whirlwind. A hypnotic chanting filled the air, 'Surin . . . Astar . . . Surin . . . Astar . . .'

'Alena!' shouted Sarah. 'Pick up the Star Stone. Quickly!'

She gave the girl a hefty shove that sent her staggering towards it. The princess gazed upon the dead goblin and the jewel. Everyone waited with bated breath. What would she do? The evil whirlwind was almost upon her.

For an agonising moment she hesitated, then making her decision she stooped to pick up the Star Stone. To everyone's relief she replaced it around her neck, and smiled.

The wind died almost instantly, and with it the eerie chant. When the small funnel of debris reached them, instead of going for the princess it hovered over the dead goblin. They watched in awe as green smoke poured upwards from his body.

Moments later, the whirlwind sped away northwards. All that remained was an empty black robe.

'Phew, that was close,' gasped Peter.

'You're telling me!' Sarah retorted.

Oswain and the princess were silent.

'I think I feel safe at last,' she said quietly.

'I think so, too.' Oswain grinned and they both laughed. Everyone else joined in.

'Where's Arca?' Andrew asked at length. 'He's surely not left without saying goodbye.'

He didn't have to wait long for an answer to that question. The eagle soon came swooping back. He carried something in his talons that he dropped at Oswain's feet.

'Ah,' he said. 'Alena, come and see this.'

The princess turned to look.

'Crow!' she exclaimed.

The bird groaned and looked up at the princess. She eyed him sternly.

'You're a traitor, Crow. You have betrayed me and caused much suffering both to my friends and myself. You are the evil servant of Surin!'

Arca towered over the hapless bird. He waited to deal

the death blow to the treacherous creature.

Princess Alena held up a restraining hand.

'Go to your master, Surin,' she commanded. 'Tell him that Alena lives to serve Elmesh. Tell him Astar is dead.'

Crow nodded meekly.

Princess Alena continued, 'As for you, you are banished for ever from our kingdom. Should you ever dare return, you will be hunted down without mercy. Now, leave at once.'

The last anyone saw of Crow was a small black dot disappearing into the north. Arca's keen eyes never left him until he passed over the distant mountains.

* * *

An hour later Peter, Sarah and Andrew, together with Princess Alena and Oswain, found themselves back at Lord and Lady Trotter's cottage. The badger was delighted to hear of the successful outcome of matters, as he put it.

'But tell me, Princess, what made you decide to keep the Star Stone after all?' he enquired.

'You know, I'm not really sure myself,' she replied thoughtfully. 'You realise, of course, that the news of who I really am – I mean was – came as a great shock. I really didn't know what I would do when I met Gublak.

'I suppose it was when he seemed to turn into Surin,' she continued. 'I knew I couldn't resist my natural father and I was about to obey him. That's where Peter so bravely came to my rescue.' She smiled at him and he fidgeted awkwardly. 'I knew then that I had real friends, people who were loyal and kind, and who would even risk their lives for me.'

'Those are the ways of Elmesh,' Trotter murmured.

Princess Alena nodded.

'I know that now,' she said. 'But there's something else, too. It dawned on me that if I gave in to Surin I would have to become like him. The Ice Maiden warned me I would turn evil if I lost the Star Stone. Suddenly, I saw what that really meant. I would have to kill Peter and Sarah and Andrew to show that I was truly following my father,' she explained. 'And that would have been only the beginning.'

'Wow! I'm glad you didn't do that,' gasped Andrew with relief.

'So am I,' she replied with a wan smile.

'What about Gublak?' Sarah added. 'Wasn't that horrendous?'

'He was destroyed by his own greed,' said Oswain. 'But he very nearly gave Surin his chance. I don't think any of us expected that whirlwind. You did well, Sarah.'

She smiled.

'I felt so exposed, so . . .' began Princess Alena.

'Well, that's all in the past,' Trotter interrupted gently. 'Now, what's next?' He glanced in Oswain's direction.

'I think we must get Alena back to Elmar as soon as possible,' he answered. 'Our parents will be very concerned and we should not delay. I will ask Arca to go on ahead and give them the good news.'

He rose to his feet.

'Can we come, too?' Peter asked. 'We've never been to Elmar.'

Oswain smiled. 'But of course. Indeed, it is high time I paid a visit myself. We shall journey together.'

*   *   *

The three children were a little sad that their stay in the Great Forest could not be longer, but throughout the rest of the day they still managed to get round to most of their old friends. All the talk was about the battle, naturally enough, and the older ones spent much time comparing it with the time when they had fought Hagbane. As is usual with such matters, the tales grew in the telling until almost everyone was a hero. Remarkably, nobody had been killed, but those who had collected wounds were paraded around as the greatest heroes of all, and here Oswain the King, who bore the sword of Elmesh, used his hands to bring healing to all who needed it. No one received more careful attention than Grumble himself.

'How can I apologise?' said Oswain. 'It was a terrible choice.'

'But the right one,' the mouse replied. He grinned. 'And for a change, believe it or not, I have no grumbles at all!'

Early next morning, after many fond farewells, the party set off on their happy journey to Elmar. It took them three days, which was quicker than it might otherwise have been, because Oswain had befriended Gublak's horses and they allowed him and his companions to ride upon their backs.

Arca had fulfilled his mission and upon reaching the gates of the city they were delighted to find the whole place in a festive mood. Banners decorated the walls and hundreds of flag-waving people lined the streets and cheered the small procession as it made its way towards the palace. The three children marvelled at their reception.

'Wow, this is all right, isn't it?' said Andrew. 'It's like being royalty.'

'Well we are, silly,' his sister laughed. 'At least Oswain and Alena are. Don't they look wonderful?'

It was not long before the company reached the palace gates, where all the guards stood to attention and saluted them. All at once they were out of the crowds and approaching the drive towards the main entrance of the palace itself.

There stood King Argil and Queen Talesanna. Princess Alena slipped from her horse and ran to meet her parents. She flung her arms around them.

'We thought you were lost, child,' sobbed the Queen. 'Elmesh be praised, you have returned.'

'You have made the right choice,' smiled her father. 'That is even better news to my ears.'

'Yes, Father,' the princess smiled through glistening eyes.

The King turned towards his son. 'Well, Oswain, are you going to sit there all day? Come down and greet your parents.'

Oswain laughed and dismounted. He went forward and grasped his father's hands warmly. He kissed his mother.

'Now, you must introduce your companions,' said the

King. 'We have heard much about them.'

The three children were brought before him and they bowed low.

'Tch, enough of that,' he said. 'I grow too old for all this ceremony. Just treat me like an uncle, will you?'

The children laughed and immediately felt at ease with the amiable old King. He put his arms around Sarah and Andrew and together they climbed the steps of the magnificent palace, while the rest of the party followed.

The King stopped at the door and turned to the others with a twinkle in his eye.

'Now come along, Alena. You go first,' he said. 'We have a little surprise for you.'

As Princess Alena entered the palace she gasped with amazement. The great hall was jam-packed with all the nobles, officials and servants of the palace, and straight in front of her was a simply enormous birthday cake. At a signal from the King the palace orchestra struck up and everyone began to sing.

The princess was quite overcome when they applauded her and didn't know what to say.

'This is to make up for the party you missed,' the King chuckled. 'Come now, everybody, let us have a really good feast. Alena has come of age and is back with us. Oswain is here, too. I am a very happy father indeed.'

Nobody needed to be asked twice and soon the great hall was resounding to the noise of cheerful conversation and the clattering of cutlery as everyone tucked in.

'Wow, am I glad we came!' Andrew garbled through a mouthful of cake.

24
Rescued!

Princess Alena's birthday party was a great success. She herself looked quite radiant and wore the Star Stone proudly as she mingled with the guests. Everyone fussed over Peter, Sarah and Andrew, especially as rumours of their exploits spread around the hall. Much to Andrew's delight there was a simply enormous amount of food and he gorged himself to his heart's content.

Oswain spent much of the time deep in conversation with his parents and the Lord Chancellor. Clearly, the full story of Princess Alena's past had serious implications for the Kingdom of the West.

'I bet Oswain's telling them everything about Alena and Surin,' said Andrew through yet another cream bun. He choked on a crumb.

'That'll teach you to talk with your mouth full,' his sister laughed. 'You'll be sick in a minute if you eat much more!'

Peter interrupted before Andrew could think of a suitable reply. 'I wonder what they'll do? Do you think they can really trust Alena now?'

'Surin might declare war, anyway,' Sarah added.

Their ponderings were cut short by the Lord Chancellor, who clapped his hands and called silence for the King.

'My lords, ladies and gentlemen,' the King began. 'Thank you all for coming to celebrate our daughter's thirteenth birthday, even though for some reason which, *ahem*, has slipped my mind, it is a little late.'

A ripple of laughter went around the hall.

King Argil continued: 'A strange tale has been told me by Oswain, the details of which I will not bore you with now. Nevertheless, many adventures have befallen our princess and great destinies have been decided as a result.'

He paused for breath.

'As you see, the Queen and I grow old and it will not be so many years before Elmesh calls us. Another must then rule the City of Elmar and the Western lands. I am proud to say there is one who has proved worthy of that honour and I would like now to name my successor.'

A small ripple ran across the room. The King waited for silence.

'By the will of Elmesh, I declare my daughter, Princess Alena, to be the lawful heir to the throne upon my departure,' he announced with a smile.

All present applauded. The princess looked somewhat abashed but pleased.

'Furthermore,' the King added, 'a highway shall be built between the City of Elmar and the Great Forest of Alamore. Resting houses will be set up along the way. As you appreciate, Alena is of tender years and there will be need of talk between her and Oswain. Who can tell what the future may hold? Yet this I know. Two swords have been wondrously forged from one fiery bond. Thus, a brother and sister shall between them hold the great lands of the East and West in the harmony of Elmesh's will. So shall all Caris Meriac dwell in peace.'

There were many cries of 'Hear, hear' to this. Oswain and Alena smiled at one another. Both carried their blades sheathed at their sides.

'One other matter remains,' said the King. 'I have been told of the exploits of Peter, Sarah and Andrew. Without their loyalty and courage, matters would have taken a very different course and I would have been a grieving father this day.

'These must soon return to their own realm. Yet I would wish them to depart with our gratitude and, should they ever come back, to be held in highest honour.' He turned to the children.

'Would you come forward, please?'

They did as they were bidden and stood before him, feeling rather ashamed of their grubby clothes.

The King sensed their embarrassment and addressed them. 'In our kingdom poor clothing is no mark of shame, especially when such garments speak of honourable deeds. Kneel before me.' He whispered, 'Have to do these things properly, you know.'

The King took a great sword from the Lord Chancellor and with it dubbed the three children in turn.

'Arise, Sir Peter,' he cried. 'Arise, Lady Sarah. Arise, Sir Andrew. I pronounce you free knights of the realm of Caris Meriac.'

There was more applause and much cheering.

'Well, well, that is all,' said the King. 'Carry on eating, everyone.'

'Hey, it doesn't half make you feel good, doesn't it?'

Andrew exclaimed. 'Fancy being knighted!' Peter and Sarah smiled to each other.

Oswain came across and offered them his congratulations. From then on, the children had a steady stream of people doing the same until they felt quite overwhelmed.

At last, they were joined by Princess Alena and her mother.

'Thank you,' the princess said simply.

Queen Talesanna looked upon Peter, Sarah and Andrew with her serene grey eyes. 'You have fought well against forces whose power is far greater than ever you could imagine,' she said in a soft voice. 'Our kingdom has been saved and our daughter restored. I do thank you.'

The King and Oswain approached. 'Well, well. What a happy day,' chortled the jovial old man. 'Now, are you staying long? The palace is yours for as long as you wish, and the freedom of the City, of course.'

'Well, actually, we'd love to stay, your Highness,' Peter began.

'But they need to return to their own realm, Father,' Oswain finished for him.

The boy nodded.

'Oh, deary me. Yes, of course. Well, how are you going to do that?'

'The Tower of Visions,' the Queen said quietly.

'Then so shall it be. We will go there at once.'

Somehow the children knew this was the right moment to depart, so they accompanied the royal family up a staircase that led into a lofty tower. They entered an empty room with seven windows set in seven walls.

'It will not be possible to return you to exactly where you came from,' Oswain explained. 'To do that would mean going down to the sea, which would take too long. But we will trust Elmesh to see you through safely.'

'Well, goodbye,' said the King. He shook hands with the boys and kissed Sarah.

Oswain and the Queen did likewise.

'It feels so sad to be going,' said Sarah. 'It would be wonderful if we could stay for ever.'

Princess Alena stepped forward. 'I hope we meet again sometime,' she said. 'You really have become good friends to me. I shall miss you.'

With that she said goodbye to Sarah and Andrew. However, she kissed Peter. 'That's for being a special friend,' she grinned. He blushed and heard Andrew chuckle behind him.

Oswain took charge of the proceedings. He indicated a lamp that hung above their heads.

'Concentrate upon the light,' he said, 'and do not be afraid. Farewell, my friends.'

The children obeyed and the room flooded with blue light. A rushing noise filled their ears and they felt themselves floating upwards into the misty light until they were drifting in a world of dreams.

The sound turned into a gentle swishing and Peter wondered why his feet felt cold. Surely the duvet hadn't fallen off his bed again? Suddenly, he came to his senses. He was not in bed, as he thought, but standing on a rock in the midst of the sea. The cold was water splashing over his feet and the sound was that of the waves. Sarah and Andrew were both there with him.

'Ugh,' cried Sarah. 'It's cold.'

'And wet,' Andrew added. 'Where are we?'

'I'll tell you,' Peter said grimly as he gathered his wits together. 'We're back, but we're stuck on a rock and we're cut off by the tide. Look!'

They followed his gaze. All around them the sea hissed and splashed. Ahead was the cliff face and they could make out the entrance to the tunnel of the round hole – but there was no way they could reach it.

'Can't we swim for it?' Andrew suggested.

'Not a chance,' his brother replied. 'We'd be smashed to pieces against the rocks.'

'What are we going to do, then?' Sarah shrieked.

'I don't know,' Peter replied.

'Look, there's someone on the cliff up there,' Andrew pointed out some small figures. 'Start shouting and waving.'

'Huh, they're only little kids,' said Peter after a few moments. 'They're waving back. They think it's a game.'

Just then another figure appeared. It looked like a man. He took one look, waved to them, then ran off.

'Phew, I think he's realised we're in trouble,' said Peter. 'He's gone for help.' Then he added as an after-thought, 'At least, I hope he has.'

'Well, he'd better be quick,' Andrew said. 'The tide's coming in all the time.'

All three scrambled to the top of the rock and waited. The waves and the spray soaked them right through and they felt very cold. Sarah noticed they were back to their light summer clothes.

'How long've we got, d'you reckon?' Andrew asked.

'Dunno,' Peter replied. 'Ten minutes or so. I've no

idea really.'

'Mum and Dad will kill us when they find out,' Sarah groaned. 'What'll we say?'

'Tell them the truth, I guess. We always do. But they'll never believe us, of course,' her younger brother replied.

Just then they heard a new sound above the roar of the sea. A steady thrumming came from round the headland. It grew louder.

'Hey! Look,' cried Andrew. 'It's a helicopter. Wave your hands.'

The bright yellow shape of an RAF Sea King whirled into view. The noise grew deafening as it banked and hovered above the cliff.

'They've seen us,' cried Sarah. 'Hooray!'

A voice barked from a loudhailer. 'Stay calm. There's no need to panic. I'm sending a man down to lift you off one by one.'

The helicopter hovered overhead and they could feel the powerful down draught from its massive five-bladed rotor. Even the waves flattened out under its force. The whine from the twin Rolls Royce Gnome turbo shafts made it almost impossible to hear anything else.

Moments later a figure appeared to step into space from the right-hand side of the machine and they watched open-mouthed as he winched down towards them. After a few trial swings he landed on the rock.

'Everyone all right?' he shouted. 'No broken bones or anything?'

'No, we're fine,' Peter yelled back.

'OK, missy,' he smiled at Sarah. 'Ladies first, I reckon. Stick your arms through here and I'll come up with you.

Won't be long, lads.'

Sarah obeyed and was soon snug in the special rescue harness. The crewman waved and in an instant Sarah was whisked off the rock. It was a scary feeling and the hawser looked very thin. She was glad the man was with her and she clutched him tightly.

The view was dizzying. She glanced down. Peter and Andrew looked like little white ants on their tiny rock and she marvelled at the skill of the helicopter crew. In a few moments, they were level with the hatch and another crewman helped them into the cabin and onto the deck.

'Mind the edge now,' he said to Sarah. 'You're safe.' He helped her out of the sling. 'All right, George?'

'OK, Bill,' said the crewman. Seconds later, he was gone again.

It took only about five minutes to have all three children winched to safety but by now quite a crowd had gathered on the cliff top. The pilot manoeuvred until his helicopter was over the grassy top.

'Stand clear. Everyone stand well back,' he barked through the loudhailer. 'I'm coming in to land. Everyone stand well clear.'

It took some minutes before he felt it safe enough to bring the great machine down. The boys especially would have loved to look all over the helicopter but as soon as they touched down and the engines were reduced to tick-over, George ordered all three out.

They were just walking clear when a man and a woman broke from the crowd and came dashing towards them.

'It's Mum and Dad,' cried Sarah.

She ran into her mother's arms.

'Oh, I'm so glad you're safe,' sobbed Mrs Brown. 'We didn't know where you had got to these last two hours.'

The boys were joined by their father. He looked grim.

'What happened, Peter?' he demanded. 'Where have you all been?'

'Sorry, Dad. We were cut off by the tide . . .'

'Of all the stupid . . .'

He was cut short by the crewman, George.

'Are you their father, sir?'

He nodded. 'I'm terribly sorry about all this. I've always taught them to be careful of the tides. I just don't know what got into them.'

'Well, it happens all the time,' George smiled. 'Good job we were in the area. Not everyone's so lucky. Anyway they're safe and sound now and that's what matters. Don't be too hard on them, sir.'

Mr Brown was a good father. He smiled back. 'No, I won't,' he said. 'But they'll get a good talking to all the same.'

While he and the crewman sorted out the details for a report, the children stood with their mother.

'I wish everyone wouldn't keep staring at us,' Andrew muttered.

'It's because you're celebrities,' his mother replied. 'After all, it's not every day you see a real live air-sea rescue. They'll soon go, don't worry. Now, tell me what happened.'

'You're not going to believe this, Mum . . .' Peter began.

* * *

The next morning, Peter, Sarah and Andrew were again walking on the cliff top. Sarah had drawn a new jewel on her tummy – it was, naturally, a shining blue sapphire. They wanted to have another look at where they had been rescued, though their father had given them very strict instructions not to descend the round hole or go on the rocks.

'I knew they wouldn't believe us,' said Andrew.

'Never mind,' his brother grinned. 'We know what happened.'

'I still wish we hadn't given Mum and Dad such a fright,' said Sarah. 'They thought we'd been daydreaming.'

'Wasn't it good in the helicopter?' said Andrew. 'I wouldn't mind doing that again.'

'Once is enough for me,' said Sarah firmly.

'I wonder what will happen to Alena now?' Peter murmured.

'I'd like to know what Surin will do,' Andrew said. 'I bet he was furious with Crow.'

'He was a nasty bit of work, that bird,' said Peter.

They reached the round hole and lay on their stomachs to peer over the rim.

'Hey, what's that down there?' Andrew asked.

They followed his finger. There, lying at the bottom of the hole, was a large black bird.

It was a very dead crow.

Oswain and the Battle for Alamore

by John Houghton

Discover the secret of Oswain's
past and the awesome power of
the Merestone.

Everyone loves an adventure
story, but it's a bit different
when you're actually part of one
– as Peter, Andrew and Sarah
find out when they climb into a
tree and end up in the Great
Forest of Alamore.

Through courage and loyalty,
laughter and tears, join Prince
Oswain and Trotter the badger
as they struggle against the evil tyrant Hagbane in this
fast-moving, action-packed story of the battle between
good and evil.

'. . . as exciting and tense as Harry Potter' – Shaun
Millward, aged 10.

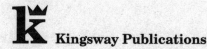 **Kingsway Publications**